My Walk With Mom

My Walk With Mom

A Diary of Events, Thoughts and Feelings

DOLLIE BLACKMON FULLER

ReadersMagnet, LLC

My Walk With Mom: A Diary of Events, Thoughts, and Feelings.

Copyright © 2021 by Dollie Fuller.
Published in the United States of America.

ISBN Paperback: 978-1-956780-32-1
ISBN Hardback: 978-1-956780-33-8
ISBN eBook: 978-1-956780-31-4

All rights reserved. No part of this publication may be reproduced, stored in a retrieval system or transmitted in any way by any means, electronic, mechanical, photocopy, recording or otherwise without the prior permission of the author except as provided by USA copyright law.

All Bible citations are from the King James Version.

The opinions expressed by the author are not necessarily those of ReadersMagnet, LLC.

ReadersMagnet, LLC
10620 Treena Street, Suite 230 | San Diego, California, 92131 USA
1.619.354.2643 | www.readersmagnet.com

Book design copyright © 2021 by ReadersMagnet, LLC. All rights reserved.
Cover design by Ericka Obando
Interior design by Mary Mae Romero

Contents

Acknowledgments vii
"Moments in Life" ix
Preface xi
Introduction xiii

Chapter 1   A New Beginning 1
Chapter 2   The Speeding Ticket........................... 19
Chapter 3   Mom's First Hospitalization............... 27
Chapter 4   The Crossroads of Life....................... 44
Chapter 5   Facing Reality..................................... 59
Chapter 6   Mom Leaves Her Home 65
Chapter 7   In Search of Services 85
Chapter 8   Mom Saw Daylight 90
Chapter 9   It's a New Year.................................. 150
Chapter 10 George has a Stroke......................... 172
Chapter 11 Mom's Spells 181
Chapter 12 Mom's Second Hospitalization........ 193
Chapter 13 Mom's Surgery................................. 204
Chapter 14 A Crack in the Sky 229
Chapter 15 Divine Peace 239
Chapter 16 My Life without Mom 244

David's Poem "I'm Free"... 249

Acknowledgments

***

First I would like to thank God for all His many blessings. I will continue to put Him first in my life because without Him, I could do nothing.

I would also like to acknowledge three people: my late husband, Clarence, and my brother, Daniel. I thank Clarence for not giving me a hard time about taking in my mother. He never complained and did whatever he could to make her life comfortable. I believe in my heart that he cared about her deeply, and with his help, I was able to make Mom believe that our home was her home also. It made me feel good that first time I heard her say, "I want to go home," especially when I knew she was talking about the home we shared. It is with great sadness that Clarence passed away on 5/7/20 from Covid-19 complications.

For years, Daniel held down the fort alone. He lives in Hemingway, South Carolina, which was over two hours from Mom's house in Chesterfield. He traveled back and forth, taking Mom to her many medical appointments, while keeping the family abreast of her condition. In addition, after I moved back to South Carolina, he was there for me whenever I needed him, and I thank him for everything.

Finally, my sister Cathy (Stacy) retired early from Yale University and relocated to South Carolina to help care for Mom. She was a big help and we all appreciated her sacrifice. She purchased a house around the corner and would be there within minutes when called. We all loved having her close.

"Moments in Life"

There are moments in life when you miss someone so much that you just want to pick them from your dreams and hug them for real! So cherish them while they are with you.

When the door of happiness closes, another opens; but often we look so long at the closed door that we don't see the one that has been opened for us.

Don't go for looks; they can deceive. Don't go for wealth; even that fades away. Go for someone who makes you smile, because it takes only a smile to make a dark day seem bright. Find the one who makes your heart smile.

Dream what you want to dream, go where you want to go, be what you want to be, because you have only one life and one chance to do all the things you want to do.

May you have enough happiness to make you sweet, enough trials to make you strong, enough sorrow to keep you human, and enough hope to make you happy.

The happiest of people don't necessarily have the best of everything; they just make the most of everything that comes along their way.

The brightest future will always be based on a forgotten past; you can't go forward in life until you let go of your past failures and heartaches.

When you were born, you were crying and everyone around you were smiling. Live your life so at the end, you're the one who is smiling and everyone around you is crying. Don't count the years—count the memories. Life is not measured by the number of breaths we take; but by the moments that take our breath away!

—**Anonymous**

Preface

***

When I wrote my first book, *Gaining Strength through Life Struggles: A Story of Survival*, I discussed my childhood and being raised in a rural community with three sisters and two brothers. Since that book was published, my mother went through a period of decline and eventually suffered serious illness and death. In this, my second book, I describe the ordeal of watching the steady decline of someone I felt would always be there and dealing with the myriad attendant problems. I hope that this book will demonstrate to others who are going through the same situation that they are not alone.

All Bible citations are from the King James Version.

Introduction

***

My Mom

This book is a tribute to my mother. She was born on February 4, 1923 in Youngstown, Ohio. She married my father on February 22, 1940, They had six children. My father died on October 2, 1985, and my oldest brother passed away on March 7, 1998.

My mother led a full, happy, and active life. She enjoyed spending time with her family and friends. She confessed Christ at an early age and joined Grove Baptist Church in Chesterfield, South Carolina, in 1943. My mother was a faithful member until she became ill and was unable to attend church services anymore. She passed away on June 6, 2010, at McLeod Hospice House.

My mother inspired me more than she knew. Whenever anything happened, she would say, "Dollie will write it down in her book." She bragged so much on my notes that I had no other choice but to keep them up-to-date. I am so glad I did. I told her often how much I loved her, and she told me frequently how she felt about me.

Mom, I tried daily to show you how much I cared because I never wanted you to think for a minute that you were a burden to me. We might not have always shared the same views, but your wisdom was something I was very proud of. Thank you for trusting me with your innermost thoughts and providing me with so much of our family's history. I thank God for all the memories.

This diary spans a three-year period that culminated in my mother's passing. It started from a desire to keep track of everything, so I wouldn't forget anything. I read some of it to my mom, and she seemed to enjoy it very much. I told her that I was writing a book about her, and she loved that idea. She wanted people to know what she was going through. Taking care of my mother was a difficult challenge for me, but the struggle was strengthened by love. We were faced with so many obstacles, some large and some small, but by the grace of God, we managed to resolve them one by one.

Although everything in this project is true, it is still from my eyes. Yes, they are views and observations flowing from my heart. I hope this book will inspire others who may be going through similar situations. Yes, it will be a challenge, but you can make it. We must always remember that God is in control of everything. We must put all of our trust in the Lord and His divine wisdom because He will never put more on us than we can bear.

Chapter 1

***

A New Beginning

"But they that wait upon the LORD shall renew their strength; they shall mount up with wings as eagles; they shall run, and not be weary; and they shall walk, and not faint." —Isaiah 40:31

April 2007–September 2007

The year 2007 brought about so many changes in my life that it was like a new beginning for me. The first change was my retirement on April 1, 2007, after working more than four decades in academia and social services. I thought this change would usher in a life without stress, but that was so far from the truth. When I thought about my working days, my life was pretty stressful at times, especially after I moved up the ladder into a management position. Nevertheless, that was my life before retirement. I remember walking out of the building my last day on the job. I was so excited that I couldn't stand myself. I was thinking, "*I did it—yes, I am now retired.*" I honestly thought my life would be a lot more relaxed.

At first I had to get used to not going to work. I had a lot of time on my hands. I was able to sleep in whenever I wanted. I could enjoy a cup of coffee while in my bathrobe, read a good book, or even write down my thoughts whenever they came to mind. It felt good having that time to myself and being able to relax and reflect on my life. Regrettably, that was short-lived. After a while my life started to get extraordinarily busy, to say the least. When you think about how quickly time passes, it can be mind-boggling. I can't believe that I retired over three years ago. Yes—I am already in the second stage of retirement.

October 2007–December 31, 2007

The second change was relocating to another state. My husband, George, and I relocated to South Carolina approximately six months after I retired. It took months to pack up everything and prepare for the move. The relocation went without a hitch, and we are still very pleased with our decision. It was a major change for us, but I thought it would be an easier transition for me because I had lived in the South for the first eighteen years of my life. Although George had never lived in a rural setting, he adjusted well to the move. Yes, I was wrong again. The truth of the matter was that George adjusted more quickly than I did.

We found a cute little house in the country near Florence, South Carolina, an hour and a half away from my mother in one direction and an hour from my brother, Samuel, in the other direction. Being in the middle of both Mom and Samuel was very convenient for us at that time. During our first year in South Carolina, Samuel helped us make a large number of repairs on our house, workshop, and landscape. He would work for hours in the heat, clearing the land, and repairing the workshop.

One day while we were working outside cutting branches off the trees, I fell hard on my back. I thought I had broken my neck at first. George had to help me up. I had been so careful during the move not to do anything that would jeopardize my fragile back. I initially hurt my back at work when a file cabinet almost fell on top of me. I ran the gamut of therapy from exercise to medication. I was at a point where I could sleep through the night without experiencing chronic pain. Unfortunately, that fall was the straw that broke the camel's back; it aggravated my back so badly that I ended up going back and forth to the doctor for months.

My brother worked on our property (house, land, and workshop) two or three days a week the remainder of the year. We also had a lot of work done on the house such as completely bricking the entire house, installing a subfloor in the living room, as well as removing most of the carpet in the house and replacing it with laminate flooring. Samuel, George, and I spent a great deal of time together. I never really liked cooking, but I cooked more during this time than I had ever cooked before in my life. I have three sisters, and only two of them liked to cook. Tracy and Gloria were the cooks. Stacy and I cooked only when we had to. We both can cook, but it was not our favorite thing to do. Yet, I found myself cooking all the time for Mom, George, and Samuel. I started to take pride in my cooking and tried using different spices and other ingredients. Everyone would brag about my food, which made me try even harder to cook well.

During that time, Samuel and I became very close. George and I would go to Hemingway and spend time at Samuel's house, and he would do the same with us. The three of us would sit around the table and talk. George and I only knew a few people we met in church. George was not as outgoing as I was, so I was glad he had another male to relate to.

I also spent a lot of time the first few months trying to find medical providers for George and me. I searched the Yellow Pages and asked people I met in the area about different doctors. We needed to find a good primary physician and a dentist.

I was able to find a young black female doctor for myself, and she was as sharp as a tack. I liked her very much. I met with her for the first time on October 26, 2007. She did a complete physical exam, and she was thorough. She immediately noticed my heart murmur and wanted me to see a heart doctor. She referred me to Advanced Cardiology Associates. I saw the heart doctor on November 29 and December 6 that year. I saw my primary physician again on December 27. I was also able to find a good doctor for George. His first appointment was scheduled in February 2008.

January 2008–June 2008

Samuel

The third change was assisting my brother to care for our elderly mother. The first few months after our move, we only went to Mom's house every other week, as Samuel was there the alternating weeks. It was easy seeing to Mom's needs at that time because she was doing well. She was still going to church on Sundays, going out to eat with her friends, and pretty much taking care of herself.

Although we were working on the house, George and I would stop what we were doing and head for Chesterfield early in the morning when it was our week. We actually enjoyed the outing, and it took our minds off everything we had to do.

When we moved south, Mom was already up in age but doing very well living alone in her house. She was able to feed herself, take a bath, and dress herself, and even cook a little. There were times when she would forget she was cooking and burn her food, but these episodes never reached a point where she endangered herself. She had bad knees, and her legs would give out without notice. My mother still washed dishes and was able to keep the house somewhat neat. I was concerned about her washing dishes leaning on the side of the sink because her legs could give out on her. Although she had a walker, she never used it. She was able to walk on her own. Mom did have minor complaints, but nothing major during that time.

While Mom was doing well, I tried to schedule all of my medical appointments to get them out of the way. I had my second appointment with my primary physician on February 20, 2008, got my colonoscopy on March 7, and my mammogram on May 1. I also scheduled George to see his primary physician on February 22. We were all set for the time being.

For a number of years, Samuel had been taking care of Mom alone. Even though Samuel and I were taking turns visiting Mom and taking her to the doctor, I wanted to take on more of the responsibilities to give him a break. He continued to handle her money and pay her bills. I took over keeping track of Mom's medical appointments and medications. Anyway, George and I enjoyed going to visit Mom, and she enjoyed having us come. Sometimes we stayed for the day or overnight or for a couple of days. It didn't matter, since we were both retired.

Thinking back, I wanted to be there for Mom. I loved my mother, and I owed her so much more than what I had given her in the past. I wanted to repay her for all that she did for me when I was growing up. In addition, there were times during my stressful periods at work when I wasn't able to carry my part of the load. I couldn't visit as much as I would have liked or call as much as I should have. There were times when some of my siblings took up the slack for me, and I wanted to give back to them because I appreciated all that they did for Mom. I was the only daughter living in South Carolina at that time, and I planned to do whatever I had to do to take care of Mom. I was determined to be there when she needed me and to tell her often how much I loved her. Looking back, I did share my feelings with Mom often and tried to show her how much I cared about her. We developed a strong bond, and I believe she knew that I would be there for her until the end.

Samuel or I would always take Mom to her medical appointments because we needed to be there to talk with her doctors. At times, Mom was unable to articulate her needs, and we wanted to be sure that the doctors knew exactly what was going on. In the past, Mom would drive herself and others around town. They would go shopping or out to eat on Sundays. The doctor eventually stopped Mom from driving, but she would drive anyway when we were not there. Mom's driving was unsafe to say the least. There were times when she drove her car in a ditch or pulled in front of an eighteen-wheeler; once she lost control of her car and drove off the road and into the woods.

Soon after I moved to South Carolina, I took Mom to one of her medical appointments. The doctor said to Mom, "You are not still driving, are you?" I asked, "She's not supposed to drive?" The doctor looked at me and said, "Would you ride with her? No—she should not be driving at all. I've told her that many times, and she knows it." I'd always thought Mom drove too fast, and I'd heard about all the incidents with her car, but I didn't know the doctor had deemed her medically unfit to drive. Mom did a good job keeping that information to herself. She didn't care what anybody said and continued to slip out and drive. She would drive herself to the mailbox or down to her stepmother Miss Bell's house. Eventually, Samuel had to move her car to his house to keep her from driving. Whenever I was home, I would always take her to the grocery store or go shopping for her myself. I tried to cook enough food so that she would have a variety of things to eat in the refrigerator. I would feed her and clean up before I returned to Florence.

When most people think of retirement, they think of a time of leisure or relaxation, a time of doing whatever they want to do or just doing nothing at all. I have always been the kind of person who wanted to stay busy. I loved working on different projects and once in a while sitting and reading a good book. I set numerous goals for myself after retirement. My first goal was to read the entire Bible, which I accomplished in 2008. My second goal was to write and publish my first book. I was able to complete and publish my first book in 2009. These were big accomplishments for me. I was always very active, and I truly believe that my energy was my saving grace.

Even though I retired expecting to relax, travel, and enjoy the rest of my life, fate had another plan for me. My aging mother, who initially seemed to have energy to spare, had one crisis after another and ended up in the hospital. This was only the beginning. After my retirement, I had moved close to my mother to help out, but as her health deteriorated, I soon realized that the move was not close enough. Some days I was driving over two hundred miles a day to take Mom to see her doctors, pick up her medication, go to the grocery store, and head back home. Soon, this began to take a toll on my body and my health started to decline. I had to remind myself that I was also a senior citizen. I asked myself, *"How long can I keep up this pace?"*

The fourth change was caring for my mother full time. Samuel and I worked together in an effort to maintain Mom in her home. However, her health went back and forth. She lost most of her hearing and had to get hearing aids. The straw that broke the camel's back was the blindness. My mother went blind in both eyes and could no longer live alone. I knew Mom didn't want to leave her home, but I also knew she could not stay there alone. Mom hinted that one of us should move in with her, but that was out of the question. First of all, the house was also weakening, and it would cost a fortune to bring it back up to code. At the time, we had to think about what was in Mom's best interests. As much as we hated facing that decision, we had to move her out of the family home.

The fifth change was to purchase another house. When Mom initially moved in with George and me, it was a big change for all of us. I prayed and asked God to give me the strength and the knowledge I needed to take care of her. I also asked Him to help us to live together in peace and harmony. Yes, we all had to learn to live with each other, and this was a challenge. I thought, *"George and I have been alone for a long time, and we know each other. He doesn't pressure me if I don't feel like cooking. We both love eating out, and we eat out frequently. I am able to sleep in when*

I want to. We are able to go any place at the drop of a hat because we don't have anyone but ourselves." Although I believed in my heart that I could do it, I still questioned myself. *"Will I be able to take good care of Mom? Will I be able to keep track of everything?"* I knew that I was taking on an immense responsibility, but I was up for the challenge. *"Lord, I need your help more than ever because I can't do this by myself."* I loved my mother, and she needed care. I didn't want to let her down because she took good care of us when we were growing up, and now it was our time to take care of her.

The first obstacle was the setup of the house where we lived. Mom had to come out of her room to go to the bathroom. This wasn't good. We wanted her to have her own space that was large enough to include everything she needed. I knew what Mom needed, but I also knew George loved the house we lived in—so did I. At first, he did not want to hear anything about moving. However, we both knew that house wouldn't work with Mom. We both agreed to do what we had to do. We eventually put our house on the market and purchased another house that was more adaptable to all our needs.

Taking care of Mom full time also meant that I had to keep track of all her finances (Samuel quickly gave that up after Mom moved in with me), her appointments, medications, bills, and daily needs. I was already taking care of George and myself. Could I do it? I tried to be positive. I remember saying to myself over and over again,

"*Yes, I can do this.*" This was a big change for me, but I was able to adjust my life to the change. Mom, George, and I worked together. With the help of the Lord, everything fell into place.

Dollie's Diary

***

June 27, 2008

Today I drove to Chesterfield to pick Mom up for a follow-up visit with her primary physician Dr. Mason. She complained of swollen toes and joint pains. When the nurse took her in to check her vital signs, she asked my mother how she was doing. My mother answered, "I feel just as good as you do." When I heard my mother say those words, my mind took me back to the car ride from home to the doctor's office. My mother had told me only minutes earlier that she hurt so badly at night she couldn't sleep. She complained about the pain she was having in her toes and her knee. Mom went on to tell the nurse she needed surgery on her left knee, and the doctors wouldn't operate. I stepped in and reminded Mom that having surgery on her knee was too risky because of her health and age, and that the doctors said she may not live through the surgery.

I immediately changed the subject and told the nurse what my mother had said to me. She wrote it down and said that the doctor would check it out. I was glad to hear my mother speak more positively about the way she was feeling because she could be very negative at times. However, we were in the doctor's office, and the only way the doctor could treat her symptoms properly was to know what they were. The doctor came in and checked my mother. The swollen toes were most likely from her arthritis and diabetic pain. He increased her Neurontin from 100 mg to 300 mg to help with the joint pain. He also prescribed a knee brace. Mom weighed 193 pounds on this date. This weight was significant to me because she seemed to be losing weight pretty fast. In the past, Mom weighed over 250 pounds, and she wore clothing size 26W. Another thing, my mother was only five feet, two inches tall. Yes, my mother needed to lose weight, but she had never managed to lose any in the past. Now she'd lost over sixty pounds in less than a year; to me this was major because she wasn't trying to lose, and she had an enormous appetite. After leaving the doctor's office, I stopped by the pharmacy to fill her prescriptions. We got the knee brace and the medication. I took my mother home and made her a nice dinner. Mom ate well. It was clear that nothing was wrong with her appetite. I made her a plate for later and put it in the refrigerator. Mom did well the remainder of the month. Samuel and I continued to visit weekly.

July 1, 2008

The month of July started off well. Mom was feeling good and had a lot of energy. Mom was excited because her babies were coming home.

July 17, 2008

My two baby sisters, Stacy and Tracy, are twins. They both came home to see Mom for a couple of weeks in July. Stacy lived in Connecticut and was on vacation from Yale University. Tracy lived in North Carolina and would always find her way to Chesterfield when Stacy was home. It was a twin thing. They were very good with Mom—extremely patient and caring. In fact, they spoiled her rotten. Mom enjoyed being the center of attention. Mom always enjoyed her children coming home to spend time with her. She was beaming and very happy. Stacy and Tracy were able to get Mom to come to Florence to see me. I didn't know how they did it, but Mom came. Mom had been very reluctant about leaving home for any significant time or distance, except for church or to visit with some of her widowed friends. We cooked outside on the grill, and Mom loved sitting under the carport with everyone. However, she didn't want to stay long. Stacy immediately took Mom back home when Mom got ready to go. Otherwise, she would never be able to get Mom to go anyplace with her again.

July 18, 2008–July 20, 2008

While Stacy and Tracy were home, we decided to take Mom to Tracy's house for the weekend. Mom really wanted to go, as she wanted to see Tracy's house. We drove George's van, so she could be comfortable. Tracy left her van at Mom's house. Mom tolerated the three-hour ride to North Carolina very well. We stayed a few days to give Mom a chance to rest up. She was able to see all of Tracy's children and grandchildren. We all enjoyed the trip.

July 21, 2008

Stacy stayed with Mom for a few more days after we returned from North Carolina. While she was there, she took Mom to see her primary physician. Mom started having bladder problems. There were times when she couldn't make it to the bathroom. Mom was a proud woman. Not making it to the bathroom was extremely difficult for her, and she was embarrassed. We knew she couldn't help herself, as her bladder got weaker by the day. The doctor checked my mother and referred her to a specialist to treat her weak bladder. The appointment would be scheduled by the nurse. For years, my mother took medication to treat her nerves. Her hands would shake so badly at times that she was unable to get the food to her mouth before it dropped off the fork. Mom's doctor felt that her shaking might not be nerves and referred her to a neurological specialist for shimmers. My mother weighed 195 pounds.

July 22, 2008

Stacy returned to Connecticut, and Tracy went back to North Carolina. Mom seemed to be doing okay this week. Mom had a home health aide for ten hours a week. The aide was at Mom's house for two hours a day Monday through Friday. She assisted Mom with her bath, and did some light cleaning and cooking. I had been trying to get the aide for more hours for Mom. I called Mom's case manager and requested nine companion hours. I also requested meals on wheels for Mom. I called the home health aide to see if she was willing to accept the companion hours if they were approved. She said she would accept the hours. The case manager said she would put the orders in and would get back to me.

July 23, 2008

I received a telephone call from the nurse informing me that Mom had been scheduled for medical appointments on July 29 at 10:45 A.M. with the urologist and August 13 at 10:30 A.M. with the neurologist.

July 29, 2008

Earlier this morning, my mother got sick and called Life Line herself. This was progress for Mom because she always forgot that she had the button around her neck.

She was taken to the emergency room by the emergency medical technician (EMT). The hospital staff checked her and diagnosed her with constipation. She was given medication and sent home. I was scheduled to take Mom to see the bladder specialist today, so I was already en route to Chesterfield. When I found out she was at the hospital, I went to the hospital to check on her. When I got to the hospital, I was told that Mom had already been sent home. I drove to her house, and she was sitting in the den watching TV. I asked her how she was feeling, and she said her stomach bothered her. The doctor said she was constipated. I made sure she took her medication, fixed her something to eat, and put her to bed. I stayed overnight to make sure she was doing okay. Because of the trip to the emergency room, Mom missed her appointment with the bladder specialist, so I called her doctor to reschedule the appointment. I also missed my mammogram, as I was due back in Florence in time for the appointment. I called to reschedule my appointment.

Chapter 2

***

The Speeding Ticket

"Cast thy burden upon the LORD, and he shall sustain thee: he shall never suffer the righteous to be moved." —Psalm 55:22

August, 2, 2008

I was sitting at home doing little things around the house when the telephone rang. I answered the phone, and my mother was on the other end. I said hello and asked how she was doing. I heard her faint voice say, "Dollie, I'm sick—I need you." I told her, "I'm on my way." I dropped everything, picked up my overnight bag, my pocketbook, and keys, and I was driving out of my driveway within minutes. I was now retired, and my husband and I relocated to South Carolina to be closer to my mother. Since my mother was up in age, I always kept an overnight bag packed and ready in case of an emergency. I told George that my mother was sick, and she needed me. He was unable to go that day, as we expected someone to work on the house, and someone had to be at home.

Someone once said to me, "Your health is your true wealth." Believe me, that is a true statement. We often take our good health for granted. We need to cherish every minute of good health that we have because life and good health are too short and far between. My mother lived sixty-four miles from my house, and it took me approximately ninety minutes to get there, depending on traffic. I had to drive through several small towns, which could be time consuming, to get to Mom's house. As I drove through one of the towns, I noticed flashing lights behind me. I looked in the rearview mirror and a policeman waved me over.

I stopped, and when the policeman approached the car, I asked, "What did I do?" He stated that I was speeding and asked for my license and registration. He also asked if I had seen the speed limit sign, which indicated forty miles per hour. I didn't see anything, but I always abide by the speed limit. I was shocked, but to tell the truth, my mind was not on my driving because the only thing I could think about was that my mother was sick, and I needed to be there. The officer took my information and went back to his car to call it in. When he returned to the car and said that he had to give me a ticket, I burst into tears. I was crying so hard that I could not even speak. In fact, I was almost hysterical. It was so bad that I felt sorry for the officer. He obviously felt sorry for me also because he apologized to me for having to give me a ticket instead of a warning. He stated that I was caught on camera going ten miles over the speed limit. I heard what he was saying, but my mind was still focused on getting to my mother's house. The only thing on my mind at that time was my sick mother lying there alone. I took the ticket and sat in my car for a few minutes to regain my composure. I then proceeded to my mother's house.

My mother was eighty-five years old at the time and had been sick for a few weeks. She had knee surgery on her right knee some years ago and had a rough recovery. She was scheduled to have surgery on the left knee, but because of her age, diabetes, and other health issues, the doctor felt that surgery presented too great a risk. My mother's left knee socket was gone, and she would frequently fall. A few weeks prior, she started having problems with her stomach and a weak bladder, and when she ate she felt as though she would bring her food back up. She was taken to the emergency room by the EMT on July 29, but the emergency room doctors said she was only constipated. She was sent home on medication. The medication seemed to help at first, but she continued to have pain in her stomach and had problems digesting her food. I prayed for her to be all right. I knew that prayer made the difference. I prayed and cried all the way to my mother's house. I didn't know what condition my mother was in. All I knew was that I had to get there as quickly as possible.

When I finally reached my mother's house, two people from her church were sitting with her in the den. My mother looked so frail and weak. So much so, that I almost did not recognize her. She was trying to eat some chicken noodle soup that the ladies had warmed up for her. I immediately got her dressed and took her back to the emergency room. After we reached the hospital, I helped my mother inside and parked the car. In the process of checking my mother in, she suddenly screamed out in pain. I ran to her and asked if she were all right. She said that she had a sharp pain on the side of her head. She grabbed her head and almost fell out of the chair. I thought she was having a stroke. I screamed for help.

I was so upset because not one medical staff came to my mom's rescue. I had to go get a nurse. The nurse finally came out and took her into an examination room. A staff doctor came in and checked her vital signs, took blood, and did a CAT Scan. After about an hour, a staff doctor came into the room and said, "We got the test results back, and they are all normal. We found nothing wrong with your mother." I told the doctor, "Look at her. Do you see how weak she is? Something is wrong with her!" The sharp pain in her head frightened me because my husband and daughter both had aneurisms a few years ago and both started with a severe headache. I really wanted them to find out what was wrong with my mother.

Mom was extremely weak, having muscle pain, and had what looked to be a stroke in the waiting room, yet the emergency room doctors gave me the impression that she should not have been brought back there, as she was just there four days earlier with the same symptoms. As far as I was concerned, the sharp pain in her head was new and should have been explored further. However, Mom told the doctor that she had those sharp pains before at her house. She said she fell and hit her head on the side of the bed the beginning of the year, and her head had been hurting off and on since then. Yes, Mom had fallen in the past, and yes, she had experienced headaches, but her doctor treated her for congestion and sinus infections with antibiotics. Those issues were resolved. The sharp pains seemed different to me. The doctors said to continue to give her the medication she had gotten earlier and follow up with her primary physician next week. They felt that Mom was not in danger because her test results were normal, but I knew something was wrong. I was so angry leaving the ER with Mom that I couldn't even speak. I took Mom home and made her something to eat. I called George and told him I needed to stay overnight because Mom should not be left alone. I also called Samuel and brought him up-to-date.

The next day Mom was still very weak. I continued to give her the medication she had gotten from the hospital on her initial visit, but the pills weren't working at all. I know it takes time for medication to get into your system before it starts to work, but Mom was getting worse instead of better. In fact, she got so weak that she could not turn over in bed. She was at a point of not eating anything at all. She could barely walk, and we were unable to leave her in the house alone. My brother and I took turns staying at the house around the clock because we were afraid to leave her alone. I tried to keep my other siblings abreast of Mom's condition. I kept calling Tracy to see if she could come and help us out, but she was unable to come at that time.

Early one morning during my shift at around 3:00 A.M., I heard my mother calling me. During that time I stayed awake all night anyway because I was afraid to fall sleep. As soon as I heard her voice, I jumped out of bed and ran to her room. She was half on and half off her portable toilet. I asked Mom, "Why didn't you call me?" Every night I would tell Mom to call me if she needed anything. Did she call? No, she didn't! It took me forty minutes of lifting, pulling, and tugging until I finally got her turned around and on the seat. Mom was so weak that she could not help lift herself up at all. I tried everything I could to help her. Believe me—it was almost impossible with my bad back. I don't know if a person with a good back could have lifted her that night, as she was like dead weight. I had two herniated discs in my back. I had been told by my doctor not to lift anything heavier than a remote, and my mother weighed over one hundred and ninety pounds at that time. It was a difficult night. I prayed for strength because I knew I had to help her get back in bed. Mom was sick, and I hated seeing her that way.

I stayed with Mom until Samuel arrived. Late that night, Samuel heard Mom calling him. He jumped up and ran to the room and found Mom half on and half off the bed. He also asked Mom, "Why didn't you call me?" Mom was very sick and extremely weak, but she still tried to get in and out of bed herself. Samuel helped Mom on the portable toilet and told her to call him when she wanted to get back in bed. He gave her some privacy and stood outside her door so that he could hear her. All of a sudden he heard her calling him. He went into the room and found Mom again, half on and half off the bed. He told her, "Mom, I told you to call me." Samuel helped Mom back into bed.

The next day Mom seemed to be a little better, but she was still weak. We thought that maybe the medicine was finally working. Not so. The next morning Mom was worse than ever. Samuel and I talked about it and felt that if Mom didn't get some medical treatment, she was not going to make it. Mom's doctor was still on vacation, and we knew that we did not want to take her back to Cheraw Hospital. We had called Tracy a few days before and told her that Mom was not doing well, and we needed her help. At that time, she was unable to come, but said she would call me back if her situation changed. I asked her to please come because we could not leave Mom alone at all. Samuel and I were staying at Mom's house around the clock. We had to lift her on and off the bed. We had to put her on the portable toilet. We almost had to feed her because of her weakness. I thought, *"We are losing her."* Stacy and Gloria were in Connecticut working. The only ones not working were Samuel, Tracy, and myself. It was up to us to hold down the fort. Samuel and I were there, and we were both exhausted. We needed Tracy more than ever. Tracy called that night to check on Mom. I brought her up-to-date on Mom's condition. Tracy said she had made arrangements to come and help for a couple of weeks. I was so pleased to hear those words. I called Samuel and gave him the news. Even though he had his doubts, he was also glad to hear that she was coming. Tracy told me that she had planned to come right away, which was great. I thought, *"I really hope she comes this time because we really need her help."*

Chapter 3

***

Mom's First Hospitalization

August 5, 2008–August 9, 2008

Samuel was still at the house with Mom. Samuel and I talked about Mom's condition because her health was declining fast. We had to take her to the hospital, or she was not going to make it. We made a decision to take her to McLeod Hospital in Florence. Samuel made arrangements for Mom to be transported by ambulance. My sister Tracy followed through and got there just in time to follow the ambulance to the hospital. I met them there. We arrived at the hospital around 6:00 P.M. They examined Mom and ran test after test. Finally around 11:00 P.M., the hospital doctor came into the room and stated almost triumphantly, "Our tests showed that there is nothing wrong with her liver, kidney, or gallbladder. Everything seems to be all right." To say the least, we were flabbergasted. We told her that that was exactly what the doctor at Cheraw

Hospital had told us, and that we had brought our mother there because after they said everything was all right, she continued to get worse. The doctor then told us that their test results did not indicate that anything was wrong with Mom. We told them that they needed to do some more tests because something was obviously very wrong. We were told that no more tests could be performed that night. We then told them to admit her until the necessary tests could be performed. We told them that we are not taking her home to watch her die.

Samuel and I were worried because we had been dealing with this for weeks. Mom was so sick. She appeared helpless as she lay there quietly. She didn't say anything, and that was unusual for Mom, as she would complain if she had to wait for any length of time. After a while, the doctor came in and said they would admit her for tests. We were all relieved.

During that week, they ran all kinds of tests (CAT scan, MRI, echocardiogram, X-rays, blood work, brain scan, nerve study, etc). Tracy stayed with me that week while Mom was in the hospital. We went to see Mom daily and started seeing an improvement in her condition. She said she felt better each day. She looked better, and you could see her strength returning to her body. She was able to walk around the room, and she started going to the bathroom on her own. I was happy to see the change. I thought, *"What if we hadn't taken her to the hospital? What if we waited for Mom's doctor to return from vacation?"* I was so glad we made the decision to get her to the hospital when we did.

The test results showed that Mom had a serious viral infection that had affected her muscles, bladder, and joints, and had caused severe weakness. She also suffered from arthritis and action tremors. One test showed that Mom had a back problem called spinal stenosis (discitis). They did not recommend surgery because the operation would be too intense for Mom because of her age and condition. The doctors said if Mom had the surgery, she might not make it through the operation. I do believe that Mom would not have lasted if she had not been admitted to the hospital and treated for that viral infection. Mom was hospitalized from August 5 through August 9. She was released on a number of medications including Prednisone. Mom was scheduled for a number of follow-up appointments with her primary physician, as well as other specialists.

Tracy stayed with Mom another week after she was released from the hospital. This was a big help for us. Samuel and I had a week break. That may sound small to some, but that's a big factor for someone driving 150 miles round trip to take care of a loved one. After Tracy left, it started all over again. Samuel and I started back taking turns with Mom. Her strength continued to return slowly. It was clear that she was in no condition to look after herself. If it weren't for us advocating for her, she would not have received the treatment she needed to keep her alive. Cheraw Hospital did not help Mom at all. They gave me the impression that I was wrong for bringing her to the emergency room for treatment. Why do you go to an emergency room? I told the doctor and nurse I thought the emergency room was there for people to seek medical treatment in an urgent situation. My mother was sick, and we needed and expected treatment. I couldn't believe the doctor asked me, "Why did you bring her back here with the same symptoms?" I got angry and said, "I am here because I need help. Why are you here?"

Dollie's Diary

***

"Father may be head of the home, but Mother is the heart of the home."

—Unknown

August 25, 2008

Samuel took Mom for her follow-up appointment with her primary physician. Mom was having difficulty walking. A prescription was written for a wheelchair. My mother was still having joint pain, and she used a particular ointment called Sore No More to ease the pain. It was pretty costly. We tried to get a prescription for the ointment, but we were unable to get one. My mother weighed 192 pounds that day.

September 1, 2008–September 30, 2008

I started having a lot of problems medically. My eyes bothered me, and the pain in my back was beginning to be unbearable. I was using over-the-counter pain medications but felt no relief at all. I also found a lump in my lower back that frightened me. I called my doctor and made an appointment to see her. She immediately referred me for an ultra sound on September 30 and a CAT scan in October 2008. I also had an eye exam on September 5.

September 2, 2008

I took Mom back to see her primary physician. Mom complained about feeling weak and had little or no appetite. She also had an upset stomach and had difficulty breathing at night. She felt as though she wanted to throw up but couldn't. In one week, my mother's weight had dropped from 192 to 183 pounds. The doctor put Mom back on the Prednisone. The doctor had received the hospital's report on Mom, which indicated that she had a series of ministrokes. I was not even surprised. Mom's doctor ordered immediate blood work. He also ordered X-rays and pelvic and abdominal scans. He stopped Mom's nerve pills, Lorazepam, and replaced her diabetic pill, Metformin, with Glipizide. He stopped her joint meds Gabapentin (Neurontn) and started Prednisone.

After leaving the doctor's office, I took Mom to the hospital lab before returning home for the blood work. I also stopped by the P&H Pharmacy to pick up the wheelchair, as they had called the day before and informed me that the chair had come in and was ready for pickup. I took it to my mom's house. Mom was happy to get the wheelchair. She called all of her friends and told them about the wheelchair.

September 9, 2008

Samuel took Mom to Cheraw Hospital for the ordered X-rays and pelvic and abdominal scans. Mom still showed signed of weakness. After my mother was released from the hospital and with her history of falling, she definitely needed continued care. Mom was able to use her new wheelchair. It was so much better with the chair, as Mom did not get as tired as she normally got at the doctor's office. Samuel stayed overnight with Mom.

September 10, 2008

George and I arrived at Mom's house this morning and stayed overnight, as Mom had an early medical exam the next day. I cooked Mom some food and made sure she ate before she went to bed. While sitting in the den, I started thinking about all the hours I had spent in that house. I was always afraid of the home and couldn't wait to leave when I left home. Even as an adult, I was still afraid to stay there alone. I honestly didn't know how Mom did it, as she was as content as a bug in a rug. She loved that house and wanted to stay there forever.

September 11, 2008

We woke up early and as usual, I smelled food cooking. Yes, Mom was in the kitchen cooking again. When I went in the kitchen, Mom had enough grits cooked to feed the entire family. I told Mom over and over again that we did not eat breakfast, but she still cooked grits, bacon, and ham. George and I had no other choice but to eat something. After breakfast, we got dressed, and I took Mom to see her primary physician to get the results of the tests. Mom weighed 182 pounds. The doctor reviewed the results of the X-rays, which showed that the right kidney had a spot or a possible cyst. He recommended an ultrasound. She had a thickness in her stomach wall, and her heart was somewhat enlarged. He stated that the shimmers could be onset of Parkinson disease. He restarted a lower dose of Prednisone for two weeks. He referred Mom for a colonoscopy and an Esophagogastroduodenoscopy (EGD). Mom's next medical appointment was scheduled for September 25 at 2:10 P.M.

September 18, 2008

George and I arrived the day before and stayed overnight. Early this morning, I took Mom for a consult with Dr. Gore. He checked my mother and told her about the procedures (colonoscopy and esophagus test). He scheduled the procedure for September 19 at 7:30 A.M. He gave Mom some Fleet Phospho-soda to drink to clean herself out. Mom kept saying, "I had this stuff before, and it never worked on me." Mom called everyone to say she was having surgery the following day. We stayed at

Mom's house that night, as her appointment was early in the morning. I gave her the liquid medication at 4:00 P.M. and 8:00 P.M. as directed. Within an hour, Mom was living in the bathroom. She said, "Dollie, this can't be the same thing I took before because it's working me to death." I laughed so hard, and Mom was in the bathroom all night.

September 19, 2008

After we got up this morning, I took Mom to the hospital for her colonoscopy and EGD. When we arrived, Miss Bell and another one of Mom's friends were waiting. Mom's sugar was 118 and her blood pressure was 91/86. Dr. Gore removed one polyp from her intestines and two polyps from her stomach. He sent the polyps to the lab to be tested. He said that the polyps in her stomach may have caused the problem with her swallowing and feeling that she wanted to bring her food back up. Tests would let them know what the polyps were and how to proceed. The doctor did not find any blockage. I was happy to hear that Mom did not have any blockage in her intestines because she often had problems with constipation. This was good news. Dr. Gore said Mom should not take any aspirins for three days. He wanted to see her back on September 25 at 3:00 P.M. After we got back to Mom's house, I fixed Mom something to eat, and we got ready to return to Florence, as we had been there for three days. Mom ate well and was getting around pretty good. She came outside and was sitting on the porch when we left.

September 25, 2008

Samuel stayed overnight with Mom last night. He took Mom to see her primary physician. Mom's polyps were benign. The polyps in the stomach were ulcers. Mom received medication for the infection in her stomach and three new medications (Amoxicillin: 500 mg capsules, Clarithromycin: 500 mg tablets, and Famotidine: 20 mg pepcid) that were to be taken until they were all gone. He did not want any refills on any of those medicines. Prednisone was to end in two weeks. New prescriptions of Prednisone were to be used if needed. He said Mom should have a colonoscopy every year.

October 1, 2008–October 31, 2008

My back had been giving me a lot of problems in the last few months. There were days when I couldn't even get out of bed. My primary physician referred me to a back specialist. On October 8, I had a CAT scan on my back. On October 10, I saw the back specialist. He reviewed the CAT scan and did an X-ray in his office. He referred me for an MRI on October 24 at the Pee Dee Imaging Center. He wanted to see me back in his office on November 5. I was given a prescription for pain medication. Because of my back problems, Samuel covered for me this month. I didn't want Mom to see me the way I was because she would worry.

October 16, 2008

Samuel took Mom for her appointment with her primary physician. Mom weighed 189 pounds. Mom complained about her toes swelling, but the doctor wasn't concerned about them. Mom said that the bladder medication was making her go to the bathroom too much at night. She was taken off the kidney medication.

November 2008

In November 2008, we noticed Mom coughing and spitting a lot. I called the doctor about the cough. Mom was scheduled to see the doctor on December 4 at 12:00 noon. Samuel said Mom was low on kerosene, so he ordered a hundred gallons this morning. The cost was $379.90. We all pitched in and paid for the oil. Mom was also having problems with her washing machine and hot water heater. The washing machine was not wringing out the clothes. Mom had to wring all her clothes out by hand. Samuel started looking for a washing machine. Samuel and George went to Mom's house to check the hot water heater.

I went back to see the back specialist on November 5. He said the MRI showed that I had spinal stenosis of the lumbar. I had two discs that were completely gone, resulting in the bones hitting my nerves. We talked about surgery, but I did not want to go that route. He told me about spinal injections. He said they were given in sets. *"What? Do you mean I had to take more than one?"* I wondered. I was afraid of needles going close to my spine, but the pain convinced me that I needed to try something. I was referred for spinal injections. He said not to take any aspirin until after the shot. I was also having problems with my heart and was referred to a heart doctor. On November 29, I met with the heart doctor at Advanced Cardiology Associates.

December 4, 2008

I took Mom to see her primary physician. Mom was in a good mood today. She complained about her bad cough. The doctor thought that the coughing might be due to congestion in her head. He gave her medication for the congestion. Mom also complained of not hearing out of her left ear. The doctor thought that this might also be due to the congestion. Mom told the doctor that she was going to the bathroom frequently. He gave Mom medication for her kidney. She also got a flu shot. Mom was not weighed today.

Mom started feeling better and started looking forward to Christmas. Samuel and I continued to check on her regularly. Mom had been saying for months that this may be her last Christmas, so she wanted everyone to spend Christmas with her in Chesterfield. The entire family had been talking about this for months. Mom was so sure this would be her last Christmas; we wanted to give her the benefit of the doubt. The entire family was to meet at Mom's house in Chesterfield this year. We also planned a big dinner and everyone was to purchase one gift for our grab-bag game. Everyone seemed to be excited about spending Christmas in Chesterfield. Who knows, this may be the last time we spend Christmas with our mother or at the family home. Mom's health had been deteriorating, and she may know something we don't know.

All month Mom talked about Christmas. She wanted everyone to be at the home. She would say, "I believe this will be my last Christmas, so I want everyone to come home this year." Samuel and I were still taking turns caring for Mom. Mom seemed very happy these days. She complained about her hearing and the cough, but she was on antibiotics for the head congestion. Hopefully this would knock it out for good. Otherwise, Mom had done very well so far this month.

December 13, 2008

I had an appointment with the heart doctor today. I was diagnosed with aortic valve disorder and referred for a coronary angiogram procedure on December 27. The procedure will be done at Carolina Hospital. I was glad the procedure was after Christmas, as I was expecting my children and grandchildren home for the holidays. It was a big Christmas for Mom as well. Everyone was supposed to meet at Mom's house this year. We were all excited about Christmas. I decorated the house and tried to have presents under the tree for everyone. I also decorated Mom's house and put up a little tree in her living room. She loved her little tree. I love Christmas, as it is my favorite holiday.

December 25, 2008

Today is Christmas. My two children and three of my grandchildren came down from Connecticut to spend Christmas with us. We woke up early and opened all our presents at the house. We had a big breakfast before heading for Chesterfield. It was an exciting day for all of us. I love being around my family during the holidays.

Mom's house was overflowing, and Mom was very happy. All of Moms' children were there. Of course, Samuel was late. Some of Mom's grandchildren, cousins, stepmother, Miss Bell, Mom's brother Brian and his daughter, and many others were present. Mom had a house full of people, and she loved it. We ate, talked, laughed, sang, and had a good time. I took lots of pictures, and we had a ball. As I look back, it was the last Christmas we spent at the family home, and we thank God that Mom was still with us through another Christmas holiday.

December 27, 2008

I had a coronary angiogram procedure at Carolina Hospital today. The heart doctor performed the procedure. I stayed at the hospital all day. When I got home, I rested the remainder of the day.

December 29, 2008

I went to the McLeod Surgical Center and had a steroid shot in my back. I was so nervous, especially knowing that a long needle was going close to my spine. George drove me there and back. After the shot, I was told to rest the remainder of the day.

December 31, 2008

This morning I received a call from my mother complaining that her cough and hearing had gotten worse. I could hear her TV, which was extremely loud. Yet my mother said that she could not hear it. Mom could not hear the telephone when it rang, so she missed some of her calls. I called the doctor before leaving home to see if he could see Mom today. I was told to have her there by 2:30 P.M. I called my mother back and told her to get dressed, as I was on my way. She lived sixty-four miles from me. When I arrived at my mother's house, the TV was blasting so loud that she did not hear me come in. In fact, she said that the TV sounded like a murmur. If I didn't have my own key, I would still be standing outside knocking right now. The heater was on, but my mother couldn't hear it. My mother was dressed, so we left to see the doctor.

Mom's primary physician irrigated her ears of wax buildup. He gave her two prescriptions, amoxicillin and Robitussin for the cough. He referred her to Dr. Dixon

(ENT) for a hearing aid evaluation and rescheduled Mom's appointment with the urologist for her bladder problem. Mom weighed 185 pounds. The doctor wanted to see Mom back in three weeks. Mom was very tired when we got home because we had to wait over four hours before she was seen by the doctor. There were over twenty patients in front of us. I fixed Mom something to eat and put her to bed. I stayed the night because it was too late to drive back to Florence and I was also tired.

Chapter 4

***

The Crossroads of Life

"Trust in the Lord with all thine heart; and lean not unto thine own understanding. In all thy ways acknowledge him, and he shall direct thy paths." —Proverbs 3:5–6

I was always told that stress would kill you, and it will. One morning I noticed that I was hurting all over. Everything ached. It got worse and worse as the days went by. Eventually I had to go to the doctor hoping for some kind of relief. He checked me, took blood, and later diagnosed me with rheumatoid arthritis. It was bad enough hearing *arthritis*, but the doctor went on to say that most of it was due to my age—now, *that* hurt. That's not all. One morning I looked in the mirror and saw a strange old person looking back at me. I thought to myself, "*How long did I sleep?*" If this has not happened to you, wait awhile. We all get to that stage. There are some who will get there sooner than others. Yes, before you know it, you have reached the crossroads of life—you are now a senior citizen. Your steps become slower, and you have a difficult time getting around. Your legs begin to give out on you, and you fall a couple of times. Yes, those golden years will definitely creep up on you.

In one of my former positions as a social worker, I was required to learn the different stages of life. After I left the job, I couldn't remember any of them. I had to refresh my memory and it reminded me of the saying, "out of sight, out of mind." Knowing the stages helped me service various families by understanding relationships, finances, and all other elements of living. Every person undergoes key changes in life. Although the intensity may vary from person to person, every significant transition in life has characteristics with potential turning points. When you think about the stages of life and how they relate to each individual, it helps us understand what our parents are going through when they reach a point in their lives when they feel helpless.

My mother would often think about the past and all the things she did as a young woman. In her mind, she felt like she could still take care of herself and us. It got to a point when we couldn't tell her when we were coming home for a visit because she would try to cook everything in the house for us to eat. She wanted to cook, clean, and take care of the house, but she was not able. If we acted as though she couldn't do something, she was quick to say,

"I am not helpless." I never wanted her to feel helpless, so I tried not to send such a message.

We all learn from our parents and grandparents. They strengthen our personal growth as we move through our lifecycles. When I was growing up, there were six of us—four girls and two boys. We all had different personalities and philosophies of life. In fact, we were so different that some of us could have been born to different families and switched at birth. God creates different types of people, and all are His handiwork. We need to celebrate and delight in the differences.

Year two started off with a bang. My mother's health continued to deteriorate. Things must have been going too well because the change shocked me. I thought, *"Am I taking life for granted?"* I always tried to take one day at a time because tomorrow is not promised to any of us. We must all face reality; we will all get old unless the good Lord calls us home early in life. Whatever your future plans may be, life can take a different turn quickly. Before you know it, you are living in your golden years and that life you planned is nowhere in sight.

When I think about my mother in her golden years, my mind goes back to the earlier years when she took care of her family. My mother devoted her life to caring for her family, and now it was our time to take care of her. You may think you have it made, especially since your own children are grown and doing well. They have good jobs and families of their own. What do you do when you live alone and have no one to call for help but your children? You don't want to bother them, but what else can you do? You need help. This is a clear example of how the parental role can reverse as we get older—a parent becomes the child, and the child becomes the parent. Your parents raised you, and you get married and raise your children; then your parents are unable to take care of themselves, and yes, you step in and care for them.

I know that caring for an aging parent can present difficult challenges for anyone. Even if it is staring you in the face, and you have time to plan it out step by step, it can still be devastating. You may say you can handle whatever comes, and you may be able to, but when it hits home, and you are personally faced with the responsibility of caring for another individual, whether it is an aging parent, partner, child, or friend, it can be challenging.

When I think about my life, and all that the Lord has brought me through, I simply think about His goodness, and He gives me the strength I need to get through whatever situation I face at the moment. When I feel my load getting heavy and my feet are sinking in the sand, I look to the hills from which cometh my help because I know for myself that all my help cometh from the Lord. I often thought about this song by James Cleveland:

I don't feel no ways tired,
I've come too far from where I started from.
Nobody told me that the road would be easy,
I don't believe He brought me this far to leave me.

—written by Curtis Burrell

Yes, my story is simple but true. I have reached the crossroads of life, and I thank God for bringing me to this point in time. I am not worried about tomorrow because God will see me through any obstacles that come my way. All I have to do is wait on Him.

"I wait for the Lord, my soul doth wait, and in his word do I hope." —Psalm 130:5

I got back into my routine after my mother started feeling better. I was able to return home and felt that she was well enough to be in her home alone. She had many follow-up medical appointments, but my brother and I took turns transporting her back and forth to the doctor. Every month I did her grocery shopping and made sure she had everything she needed for that month. My mother was very appreciative, and I didn't mind doing whatever I could to make sure she had what she needed. I often cut her nails and combed her hair. I made her favorite meals and made sure she had her favorite snacks in the house. My mother had high blood pressure, diabetes, a heart condition, and a bad back. She was on a number of medications that had to be kept up-to-date. My brother had been managing her finances and paying her bills when she lived in her own home, but as soon as she moved in with me, he turned that responsibility over to me.

Dollie's Diary

***

January 5, 2009

Samuel ordered another 100 gallons of kerosene for Mom. The cost was $309.90. Mom was on a fixed income and was unable to keep kerosene in her tank. We had agreed that we would all pay for the kerosene. Samuel was able to find Mom an inexpensive washing machine. Samuel bought the washing machine and took it to Mom's house. Mom was so happy to get that washing machine that she washed for days. I kept telling Mom to let the home health aide wash her clothes, but she would still wash and hang the clothes out on the line herself. Stacy and I reimbursed Samuel for the washing machine, as it was our gift to Mom.

January 12, 2009

Today I drove over two hundred and twenty five miles taking Mom to Dr. Dixon (ENT specialist) in Hartsville, PHS Pharmacy in Cheraw, the grocery store, and back to her house. Mom continued to have problems with her left ear. She was seen by her primary physician on December 4, when she initially started complaining. She was also coughing a lot more right now and appeared to be somewhat congested. Her primary doctor thought that the congestion might be the cause of her hearing loss. At that time, he irrigated her ears of wax buildup and gave her two prescriptions, Amoxicillin and Robitussin for the cough. She also got a flu shot.

Mom's hearing continued to deteriorate. On this day, she was unable to hear anything out of her left ear and only a mumble out of her right ear. Her left eye was blurry, and she still had a dry cough. I told the doctor that my mother was still on antibiotics from December 31. However, she only had four pills left. Dr. Dixon checked my mother's ears, did a minor hearing screen, and also put something down her throat to check her lower throat and nose. He found swelling in both sides of her nose and stated that he wanted to treat the symptoms before he ordered the full battery hearing test. He prescribed an aspirin a day, Nasonex nose spray, Singulair to kill the infection, and gave Mom a steroid shot. He scheduled Mom for the full battery of hearing screening tests on February 2 at

9:30 A.M. After we got back to Mom's house, I fixed her something to eat, fed her, and cleaned the kitchen before driving back to Florence.

January 26, 2009

I had an appointment with my back doctor today, and he referred me for my second injection in my back. I was diagnosed with degeneration of the lumbar, which meant that a lot of my back problems came with age. How do you like them apples? My second injection will be on February 3.

February 2, 2009

Mom was transported to Dr. Dixon's office in Hartsville by Logistics Medical Transportation. I met her there. Mom had a full battery hearing screen. The test showed Mom's hearing was way down in both ears. She was recommended for two hearing aids if possible and one if not. He wanted to see Mom in three months. Mom was referred for a hearing aid evaluation at the Hartsville Clarity Hearing Center. After Mom's examination, I drove her home. I cooked Mom something to eat, fed her, and washed the dishes.

Samuel and I ordered another 100 gallons of kerosene for Mom. The cost was $289.90. We called Curtis Oil

Company, and the total bill was over $979.00. We all agreed to pay for Mom's kerosene. The cost of maintaining Mom in her home was becoming expensive. Mom was only receiving Social Security and some food stamps. The food stamps were not nearly enough to feed her. Some months I was spending well over two hundred dollars to purchase things for Mom's house. Stacy would always send money home to help, and I know Samuel was spending quite a bit of money every month as well. I was extremely tired driving back to Florence. As soon as I got home, I took a shower and went to bed.

February 3, 2009

I got my second injection in my back today. After the shot, I stayed in bed the remainder of the day. I was finding that the shots were not helping very much. I knew I did not want to go through surgery, so I continued to take the medication and get the shots.

February 4, 2009

Today, Mom was eighty-six years old. Samuel, Tracy, George, and I surprised Mom at her house in Chesterfield. My ex-sister-in-law baked Mom a special birthday cake. It was beautiful, and Mom loved it. Samuel, Tracy, George, and I sang happy birthday to her, and she was really pleased. We cooked a special meal for her and gave her presents. We actually had a good time. Mom was beaming.

Mom at the age of eighty-six years old

"A mother's children are portraits of herself." — Unknown

February 16, 2009

I received a telephone call from Mom's home health aide stating that Mom couldn't hear out of her left ear at all. Also, when she got up this morning, she could barely see out of her left eye. I told her that Mom had a medical appointment the following day. I would alert the doctor, so he could check her out.

February 17, 2009

Overnight Mom lost sight completely in her left eye. She could hardly see out of that eye yesterday, but today she was unable to see at all. Mom was transported to the Hartsville ENT Office by Logistics. When Mom reached the office and got out of the van, she said, "Dollie, I can't see a thing out of my left eye." I noticed that she still had that bad cough.

On this day, Mom had a full hearing aid evaluation at the Hartsville ENT Office. I was surprised when the doctor said that the hearing aids cost $800 each. Although the price included warranty, office visits, and a three-year supply of batteries, it was still more than my mother could pay. To my surprise, I was told that Medicare and Medicaid would not pay for anything toward the hearing aids. I was told that there were cheaper aids, but they did not provide them. The cheaper aids were not digital or programmable. Even though I didn't have a clue where we would get the money to pay for the aids, I still allowed the doctor to make a mold of Mom's left ear, in case we could buy at least one for now and the other later. I was told that we could make payments through Care Credit or apply for help through the Hear Now Program. The application fee was $100 per hearing aid to apply for help.

After taking Mom back home, I called Carolinas Center for Sight regarding Mom's sudden loss of sight in her left eye. I was worried about her sight loss. Since it was so late, he agreed to see Mom first thing in the morning (February 18 at 8:00 A.M.). I was told that she could have a detached retina. Since Mom had such an early appointment, I brought her home with me in Florence, and she spent the night.

February 18, 2009

Mom had an appointment with the eye doctor today. He said that Mom had a stroke in her left eye. He stated that it could be hardening of the arteries or inflammatory disease, which could take out the other eye if not treated. Hearing that made me worry even more. What would Mom do if she goes totally blind? The eye doctor said he needed to rule out the inflammatory disease and wanted an immediate blood test at McLeod Hospital. It was unknown if the sight and hearing problems were related; further testing was needed. It was unknown if the left eye could be restored, but right now his focus was on trying to save the right eye. He would review the test results to rule out the inflammatory disease. Mom signed releases for him to get a copy of the MRI (August 2008) at McLeod Hospital. Mom had an OCT (X-ray of eyes) and was scheduled to see the retina specialist the following week (February 23 at 11:00 A.M.). When we left Carolinas Center for Sight, I took Mom for a blood test at McLeod

Hospital in Florence, South Carolina. I knew Mom was as concerned as I was.

The next few days, Samuel and I stayed close to make sure she was all right.

February 23, 2009

Mom saw the retina specialist, today. He reviewed a copy of the blood work, and it was okay. She did not have the inflammatory disease, and she did not have a detached retina. My mother had an eye exam, X-rays (with and without dye in the eye), and lots of photos of the eye and behind the eye. Mom was scheduled for testing of a coronary artery, the carotid artery of the neck, and heart arteries at McLeod Hospital on February 26 at 9:30 A.M. Mom was to be tested for blockage in her arteries. If there were no blockage, they could remove the cataract in the left eye.

I also saw my back doctor today. My back was still giving me a lot of problems. The lump was still there and a little sore. My doctor gave me a local injection in the lump. It felt better for a few days.

February 24, 2009

Samuel took Mom to see her primary physician for her bad cough. She was given a stronger cough syrup and more antibiotics. If the new medication does not work, he will refer her to a specialist. While Samuel took Mom, I stayed home to contact various agencies regarding hearing aids for Mom.

I felt as though I were drowning. It took a lot to keep up with all that had to be done for Mom. Between Mom, George, and my appointments, I had to start making a to-do list. Mom was having a hard time hearing anything we said. She couldn't hear the TV, and it was out of the question for her to try to talk with someone on the telephone. Samuel spoke with someone in Chesterfield about free hearing aids and got an application. He completed the application, and we submitted it, but nothing came of it. I also called various agencies regarding hearing aids but received no help at all. I called Starkey Hearing Foundation regarding their program. They gave me information regarding the application process and said Mom appeared to be eligible for their services. I started gathering all the necessary paperwork in an effort to get the application in as soon as possible. I called Hartville Clarity Center and requested a copy of the hearing test. Samuel picked the report up after leaving Mom's house and brought it to me. I went to the bank and requested copies of all the bank statements missing from Samuel's batch. I completed the application and submitted it along with nine months of banking statements, a copy of hearing screening test, and the $200 application fee. Stacy gave me a hundred dollars, and I paid the other hundred dollars for the application. I also called and requested an amplified phone for Mom.

I was feeling somewhat stressed from all that I had going on at the time. I prayed all the time for strength, and strength is what I received from the Lord. At that time, I didn't really have time for myself. In fact, I was neglecting me. For months, I had been missing some of my doctor's appointments, and I was so tired. I needed to get organized and be better at keeping track of everything in a more efficient way.

Chapter 5

***

Facing Reality

"Honor widows who are really widows. But if any widow has children or grandchildren, let them first learn to show piety [respect, reverence or obligation] at home and to repay their parents; for this is good and acceptable before God." —1 Timothy 5:3–4

After a while my life began to settle down a little. It was strange not going to work every day, but once I got used to not working, I was in seventh heaven. I loved being at home. One morning I woke up as usual, as it was just another typical day at home. After getting dressed, I poured myself a cup of coffee and stood in the sunroom looking out. It was such a beautiful day. The sun was shining, and there was a slight breeze in the air. I always loved spring weather. It was my favorite time of the year. I loved seeing the new leaves on the trees and smelling the flowers as they blossomed into the many colors of spring. I could feel the air through the screen windows. The air smelled so fresh and clean. Thank God for life, health, and strength—what more can I ask for?

I opened the door and walked outside. I was standing under the carport not even a minute before the neighborhood cat I inherited ran toward me and wrapped himself around my legs. The cat was there when I purchased the house. No matter how hard I tried to get rid of that cat, he would not go away. That cat was so spoiled, as all the neighbors fed him, yet he was always hungry. I looked around in time to see my neighbor go by on his way to work. We waved at each other. I could hear the birds singing in the trees. Even they were happily enjoying the beautiful day. I thought, "*I love living in the country.*" It is so peaceful and quiet.

I stood under the carport for another few minutes, taking in everything. Who would believe that we would buy a house in the country next to a graveyard? If you want good neighbors, move next to a graveyard—they are the best. As I looked around, I suddenly noticed someone standing in the graveyard next to my house. It was a new grave because the tent was still up from a recent burial. I stood very still because I did not want to disturb her. I don't know how long she was standing there before I came outside, but after a moment, she turned and left. She never looked up, but I could see the tears running down her face. I felt her grief, but out of respect, I did not move nor did I speak.

Having a graveyard next to my house seemed strange to many of my friends. They often asked if it bothered me or if I was afraid to be outside at night. No, the graveyard did not bother me, and no, I was not afraid to be outside at night. It was a large graveyard covering more than two acres of land. I often saw people placing flowers on the graves. I often wondered if they recognized them when they were living. Suddenly I heard a loud noise. A young man riding a motorcycle stopped and walked over to a grave and stood for a few minutes, as though he were thinking about the person. Soon he left, but the way he kneeled and prayed before he left was touching to me. Was he praying for himself, his family, or the person he had lost? You never know what people are thinking when they pay their respects. I have lived next to this graveyard for over two years and have seen many different faces.

I sometimes sat and thought about my many losses, especially my father and brother, David. I missed them so much. My sisters and I recently visited their graves. They were buried almost next to each other, which was good. My mother often said to me, "When I'm gone, I want to be buried next to Route [my father]. I will have him on one side and David on the other side." We would always say, "Yes, Mom." Mom's burial plot was next to my father at Grove Baptist Church. My father built the church, and it was a beautiful place.

I would always love Grove Baptist Church because it was where I began my journey with Christ. Mom expected me to return to the family church when I moved back to South Carolina. She talked to me about going back to our home church many times. I told her that my season was up at Grove Baptist Church. Mom never gave up because she believed what she believed and that was that. She told me once, "Route would turn over in his grave if he knew you weren't going back to Grove." It upset me hearing that, and I did vent to Stacy and Samuel, but I told Mom that Dad would be more concerned about my soul being right. When I was young, we attended Grove Baptist Church as a family, and I will forever cherish those memories. However, George and I were adults and had to go where we felt comfortable. We joined St. Beulah Baptist Church in Florence, South Carolina. Even though we knew Mom wanted us at Grove, she accepted the fact that we were not going there and eventually said that everyone should worship at the church of his or her choice.

When I thought about myself, I felt that I was my own person. Yes, I had a mind of my own. I had two children, and they were as different as night and day. I was glad God made us different. I was glad He gave us the ability to be different and still be able to survive in our own way. That was a blessing all by itself. It takes some people longer to succeed, but as long as you succeed, it doesn't matter how long it takes.

When I was eleven and twelve years old, I couldn't wait to turn thirteen, so I could say I was a teenager. I have heard people say, "I wish I were older." Yet, when they get older, they start doing everything within their power to look younger. One day I was sitting in the doctor's office waiting to be seen, when I overheard someone say, "I love her hair." The person she was talking to asked who? She said, "The older lady in the red blouse." The room was full of people, so I decided to look around the room to see the lady's hair. I was shocked when I realized that I was the only woman wearing red. I was the older lady in the red blouse. Believe me, age will creep up on you when you least expect it. We will all get there one day, and it may be sooner than you think.

It took a while for reality to sink in for me because I was like most people, refusing to see what was in full view. I knew Mom would eventually need our help, but I honestly thought that it would be much further down the road. I was so wrong. Samuel and I did the best we could to see after Mom's needs, but it was beginning to be difficult. Mom was still adamant about not leaving her house. I have to give it to Samuel because he consistently asked Mom to move in with him, but Mom would not budge. Samuel and I talked about it and decided to do whatever we could to maintain Mom in her own home for the time being. I called Mom's case manager and requested more in-home hours, but Mom was already at the nineteen-hour weekly maximum.

My siblings and I had talked about Mom living alone. After my father died, my mother became somewhat independent. Not as independent as you or I might be but independent for her. The one thing she wanted was to stay in her own home. After all, she had lived in that house since 1947, and that house was her home. At one time she talked about moving in with Samuel, but that never materialized. Every time it got close to her moving, she would say, "No, I want to stay in my own home."

My mother was on a fixed income and received very little money from social security. She was not financially able to maintain her home alone—she needed help. Furthermore, she had a bad knee and started falling, which was another problem. What do you do when you have elderly parents who are unable to care for themselves and unwilling to leave their home? When you see warning signs alerting you to the fact that they should not be left alone, what do you do? Samuel kept saying, "We need to prepare ourselves for what could happen in the future. We need to make some alternative plans." I thought about it often. *"What kind of help does my mother need now? What kind of help will she need in the future? How do I start the process of finding in-home services and out-of-home services?"* I wondered. Of course, we wanted to make sure our mother was safe and well cared for, but what do you do when your parent refuses to move out of her home?

Chapter 6

***

Mom Leaves Her Home

> "And he stretched forth his hand toward his disciples, and said, Behold my mother and my brethren! For whosoever shall do the will of my Father which is in heaven, the same is my brother, and sister, and mother." —Matthew 12:49–50

February 26, 2009

Mom was scheduled for two tests at McLeod today. She had a carotid Dopplers and echo (Tere/T) at the out-patient hospital clinic. Mom was transported from Chesterfield to Florence by the handicapped transportation services. They were late for her appointment. George and I met Mom at the McLeod out-patient entrance. We took her in, and she had her two tests. Mom was diagnosed with an acute vision loss in her left eye.

After the tests, George and I took Mom home, as our plans were to spend the weekend with her in Chesterfield and stay until my sister Tracy arrived. Samuel and I had decided that Mom should not be left alone because of the loss of sight and hearing. When we arrived at Mom's house, the house was cold, as she had very little heat and no hot water. I was very upset. This was the straw that broke the camel's back. I had just spent an entire month with water problems at my own house. I finally had my hot water repaired, and I refused to have Mom go through what I went through at my house. I thought, *"Mom should not have to live in a house that is cold and without hot water. No, she is not going to live like that."* She needed to move out of that house right away. First of all, it was no longer safe for her to stay alone. Secondly, the house was becoming a health issue as well. I sat down and talked with Mom. I told Mom that she had to leave the house. I gave her a choice—she could stay with me or with Samuel. Samuel had been asking her to move in with him for months, but she would never leave her house. After we talked, she said that she wanted to go to Samuel's house because it was a large house and he lived alone. I called Samuel and he agreed that she should not remain in the house and it was okay for her to move in with him.

February 27, 2009

Today was a big day for Mom. In fact, it was a big day for me as well. I hated being the one telling Mom she had to move out of her home. I thought, *"How can I take her out of her home? Will she ever forgive me?"* We got up early, and I made breakfast for everyone. I finished packing some clothes for Mom and started loading the van. I walked around the house and looked at the house and the land. This was where I grew up. I started thinking about growing up in that house, swimming in the pond, running and playing cowboys and Indians, climbing all the trees, working in the garden, and sweeping the yard. Everything came back to me. I hated giving it all up, and I could imagine what Mom was feeling at that moment. She had raised her children in this house. Daddy died in this house. The house was a part of all of us, and at that moment, I felt a great loss. George and I turned everything off (heat, lights, and water) and drove away from our family home. Mom was quiet on the ride to Samuel's house. I kept thinking, *"Mom must be really hurting having to leave her home. Will she ever get over this?"* I knew she could no longer stay there, but at the same time, I felt like a villain. Mom had been living in that house for over sixty years. We both knew this day would come but never imagined it would come so soon.

Our family home

When we reached Samuel's house, we took Mom in and got her settled. We unloaded the van, and I started dinner. Mom rested for a while but soon got up and sat with me in the kitchen while I cooked. Mom said, "Dollie, I knew I couldn't stay in that house the way I am now. I could hardly see how to get to the bathroom. I didn't want you to know how bad my eyes were, but I am almost blind. I really could not see enough to get around in my own house." I told Mom that I knew she lost sight in one eye, but I thought she could see well enough out of the other eye to get around in the house. I was dumbfounded. How could I not know this? I was worried about Mom's sight, but I was also worried about her living in a house without heat or hot water. I felt bad for her. I told Mom, "You need to tell me how you feel all the time. Please do not keep anything from me because I will not be able to help you if I don't know what is going on." She said she would be honest with me from that time on.

George and I stayed at Samuel's house the entire weekend through the morning of Tuesday, March 3, to help Mom adjust to being in a different environment. When we left, Tracy was scheduled to get there within the hour. Samuel would stay with Mom until Tracy arrived. When I got home, I called Samuel's house to check on Mom and to see if Tracy had arrived. Tracy was there and had arrived about a half hour after we left.

Dollie's Diary

* * *

March 3, 2009

Mom was still unable to see out of her left eye. She wanted to have the cataract removed from that eye; she believed that when the cataract was removed, she would be able to see out of that eye again. I called Marjorie at Dr. Sampson's office and told her that Dr. Clark's office said it was okay to go ahead with the cataract surgery on the left eye. Dr. Clark would follow-up with the right eye. I went down on my knees and prayed for Mom's sight to return and for her to get some much-needed hearing aids.

March 4, 2009 and March 5, 2009

I had been trying to schedule Mom's cataract surgery for three days now. I initially called Dr. Sampson's office on March 3. I was referred to Ms. Connolly. I had been calling her to schedule Mom's cataract surgery but was unable to reach her. I have been leaving messages for two days but have received no response. I had been on the telephone nonstop for days. We were running out of options. Mom needed hearing aids and eye surgery to remove that cataract. Lord, we are asking you to intervene.

March 5, 2009

Mom woke up this morning totally blind in her right eye. Overnight, she was in total darkness. It was one thing to lose one eye, but another to lose both and be totally blind. It was a good thing my sister Tracy was there, as she had to take Mom to the bathroom several times in the night because my mother couldn't see anything. Her sight in the right eye went the same way it did in the left—suddenly. When I stopped by my brother's house, they told me about my mother's sight loss in her right eye. I was shocked. I knew right away that Samuel would not be able to take care of Mom if she was totally blind – this realization hit me like a ton of bricks. "I thought to myself *"What do we do now."* I immediately called my mother's eye specialist. Since it was so late, he suggested that we take Mom straight to the emergency room.

Tracy and I got Mom dressed, and we took her to McLeod emergency room. She was checked by the hospital doctor and a doctor from Carolinas Center for Sight. They were both given the history, and the ophthalmologist spent a great deal of time dilating my mother's eyes and checking her sight. She couldn't see anything. The hospital doctor stated that Mom had what looked to be a transient ischemic attack (TIA). The doctor also said Mom had a serious sinus infection. It was noted that my mother was already on antibiotics and had been for several months, off and on. She had a terrible cough and nothing seemed to help. The ophthalmologist said that Mom's prognosis was poor and he felt that her visual loss could not be reversed. He said that the stroke-like symptoms had damaged the optic nerve. It had something to do with the circulation in the back of the eye. He recommended that she be seen by a neuro-opthalmologist in Columbia, South Carolina. He said he would call and schedule the appointment.

March 6, 2009

Mom remained at Samuel's house. My sister Tracy was still there to help out and my sister Stacy was on her way. Tracy had to take Mom to the bathroom, kitchen, and any other place she went. She had to give Mom her bath and totally dress her. Mom could not do anything for herself, as being in total darkness was new to her. Samuel started to get worried because now Mom needed more care than he could provide. Mom was set in her ways and a little old fashioned. She would not want Samuel or any other man bathing and dressing her. The bottom line was that we needed to come up with another plan. In my mind I knew Samuel would not be able to take care of Mom now. I also knew that Mom would not want him to do it either.

March 7, 2009

Stacy arrived and started helping out. Tracy was exhausted by then and needed a break. Losing her sight was difficult for Mom. In fact, it was difficult for all of us. Suddenly being in total darkness can be frightening. It was apparent that Mom was very nervous. Stacy, Tracy, and Samuel all rallied around and cared for Mom today. I called to check on them, and Stacy brought me up-to-date on Mom's condition. She told me Mom was asking for me. Stacy said today was hard on Mom. I told her I would be there the next day. I was concerned and continually prayed for Mom's sight to return. Samuel and I have help now, but we both knew it was temporary. I thought about how it would be when Tracy and Stacy left. Since they were here for the time being, I used the time to clean my house and make some telephone calls.

March 8, 2009

I called Samuel's house early this morning to check on Mom. Samuel answered the phone and said everything was about the same. He thought it would be a good idea if we could meet to discuss what needs to happen now. I told him that I was coming to his house to see Mom anyway, so we could meet while I was there.

When I arrived at Samuel's house, I was told that Mom could see a little out of her right eye, but not well. Thank you, God, for answering my prayer. My siblings and I got together and talked about a permanent plan for Mom. Samuel clearly stated that he couldn't do it but was willing to listen to any ideas we had regarding a plan (i.e., one of us taking her versus a nursing home). We all knew Mom could not return to her house and live alone. I didn't want her to go to a nursing home, but I was unsure if I could care for her myself because of my back. I also had to consider my husband, who was also sick at the time. Stacy and Tracy were both upset and in tears. They felt that Samuel and I had already decided to put Mom in a nursing home, which was clearly untrue. The only definite decision that was made was that Samuel could not do it. I thought, *"Why would Samuel and I make a decision to put Mom in a nursing home without allowing them a chance to take her? I would never do that. I didn't want her to go to a nursing home either. Do they think this is easy for me?"* At the time, I was having a lot of problems with my back and under the doctor's care. In fact, the doctor was recommending surgery. I really didn't know what condition I would be in if I followed through with the surgery.

As soon as Mom lost her sight, I knew in my heart that Samuel could not do it, but I kept my feelings to myself. He didn't have to tell me because I knew that it would be impossible for him to care for Mom in her condition. Furthermore, Mom wouldn't let him. I thought about Stacy and Gloria living in Connecticut and working, which ruled them out. Tracy, on the other hand, was retired and lived alone. I thought, *"It should not be left up to me alone, as Tracy is also retired and available."* I expected Tracy to say she would take Mom and do the best she could, but she never said that. I honestly felt that living with Tracy in North Carolina would be better than a nursing home. I asked Tracy if she thought she could care for Mom, but she only said, "Mom wouldn't want to move so far away." She thought that the distance was an issue. I totally disagreed because distance should not be a deterrent because Mom would be in the house all the time. I believe if it came down to a nursing home versus living with Tracy in North Carolina, Mom would choose to stay with Tracy. In fact, Mom would have moved to California to keep from going to a nursing home.

Tracy said if we could maintain Mom in her home, we could find a permanent live-in person to stay with her full time. My first thought was, *"How much would that cost?"*

She said she would pay her share of the cost every month for these services. I told Tracy I heard what she was saying, but her track record of following through with things had not been good. It is easy to say what you will do if this or that happens, but following through is another story. The bottom line is someone else would have to come up with the missing funds. I would never want to get Mom's hopes up and later on have to disappoint her. She left her home once, she should not have to move back and leave it again. The important question was what would be best for Mom—to go to a nursing home or to be cared for by one of her daughters? All I knew at that moment was that I did not want her to go to a nursing home, and I didn't feel that we could afford to pay a full-time person to stay with Mom, while repairing and keeping up her house. In the back of my mind, I had been thinking about trying to care for her myself, but I had to include George in that decision. I thought, *"How can I live with myself if I don't even try."*

I left the room, pulled George aside, and asked if he would be willing for Mom to come and live with us. At first he said no, stating, "What about your back? You know I can't take care of her." I agreed with him, but what else could we do? I knew we both had health issues, and I had asked him out of the blue. He needed to have time to think about it. We both needed to discuss it and pray over it; this was a big decision. In my heart, I knew I would take her before I let her go to a nursing home. I just didn't know if I would be able to do it. I was glad we had some time because

Stacy and Tracy would be at Samuel's house for another two weeks. Mom could stay there for the time being.

March 9, 2009 and March 10, 2009

What should I do about my mom? I didn't sleep at all last night because I was thinking about Mom. I couldn't let her go to a nursing home. I talked with George again about possibly taking Mom, but he said he wanted to think about it because it was a big step. I knew it was a big decision, and I couldn't blame him at all. George had been very sick in the past and had been hospitalized several times. I really didn't know how his health would be down the road. I was currently taking care of him. I knew he depended on me to be there for him, but if I was caring for another person, my time would be split between the two of them. As for me, I was sixty-three years old and had health problems of my own. I thought, *"What happens on the days when I can't even get out of bed in the morning? If I take Mom, my life would change drastically. Can I take care of two sick people?"*

The following day George came to me and said, "If you want to take your mother in, it is all right with me. I know you don't want her to go to a nursing home and neither do I." I thanked him, but I told him I wanted to pray over it a little more before I said anything to anyone. The decision had been made—we will take care of Mom. I was somewhat relieved but also a little uncertain about my ability to care for her in my current condition.

Nevertheless, I had to trust God because with God all things are possible.

> **"The Lord is my strength and my shield; my heart trusted in him, and I am helped: therefore my heart greatly rejoiceth; and with my song will I praise him." —Psalm 28:7**

March 11, 2009

I thought, *"This is really happening. Mom will not be returning to her house."* Stacy, Tracy, and I drove to Mom's house to pack up her things. This was a difficult day for us, and I knew they were probably thinking the same thing I was thinking—no one would be living in the family home. How strange was that? I decided to tell them about our decision to take Mom. They were both very pleased. They both said if I took Mom, they would do whatever they could to help out. Stacy said she would come home during her vacation every year and take Mom to Samuel's house for a couple of weeks at a time, if Mom would stay, to give me a break. She also said she would help out as much as she could financially, so that the burden would not all fall on me. This was not a new thing for Stacy, as she always purchased most of Mom's personal things, and now she was offering to continue this practice. I thought that was very nice of her, as she didn't have to do that. Tracy said she would do anything to keep Mom from going into a nursing home. She told me she would come home once a month to take care of Mom, so that I could go to church, as she knew that was one of my concerns. I had not figured out how I could go to church on Sunday, but if Tracy came home one weekend a month, it would be a big help. I thought, *"Going to church once a month is better than not going."*

I also told them that George and I had contacted a real estate agent to start looking for another house to give Mom more space. She needed a bathroom in her room. We thought about changing rooms with her for the time being, but her room was too small for our king-sized bed. All the rooms were small, and we had no other place to put her. George and I also needed to be closer to stores, town, and the hospital. Living out in the country, we were over ten miles from a grocery store and twelve miles from the hospital and doctors. Our property was on an acre and a half of land, and that was beginning to be a little more than we could handle. We wanted to buy a house that would be better suited for all of us, and would allow plenty of space for Mom and her things. My sisters both thought that the sacrifice was great, and they said they appreciated what we were doing for Mom. We arrived at Mom's house, packed up Mom's things, and took them to Samuel's house.

March 14, 2009

I received a telephone call from Stacy this morning; she told me that Mom was having headaches again. For the first time in months, she asked for one of her pain pills. I told Stacy to watch her because we do not want her to have another stroke. I was so glad Stacy and Tracy were there with Mom. Samuel had help. I used this time to make phone calls and look at some houses.

George and I looked at more than ten houses today. When some of our relatives and friends heard we were looking for another house, they could not believe it. We loved the house we lived in. In fact, I had to convince George to start looking because he did not want to move. It was clear to me that our house would not work for Mom before we made the decision to take her. If we were going to sacrifice and take care of her, we needed to make that move. After much discussion, we both agreed to put our house on the market and look for another house that would be better for the three of us. We looked at a number of houses but found nothing we liked in our price range. After looking at more than twenty-five houses, we finally saw a house that we both liked—one that George was even willing to move into.

We found this house when we were just about to give up looking. This was a four-bedroom, two-bath home close to town and stores, and only two miles from the hospital.

The yard was small enough for us to take care of. The only drawback was that it needed some work, and it had a swimming pool. I knew nothing about taking care of a swimming pool. If we got the house, Mom would have the master bedroom with the bathroom. As soon as I walked through the house, I could see Mom in that room. We put a bid on the house, and now we were waiting to hear from the seller.

March 16, 2009

Mom had a follow-up appointment with the retina specialist at Carolina Center for Sight. My brother and sisters took her to this appointment. I stayed home and called Mom's primary physician and her ENT doctor for a prescription for antibiotics for Mom, as she was still quite congested and was complaining about headaches again. To my surprise, they both called in a prescription. Both doctors were aware of her condition and had previously given her antibiotics for the viral infection.

We heard from the real estate agent. The seller accepted our bid. The agent said that she would schedule the inspection, and she later called back and said the inspection is scheduled for next week.

March 17, 2009

Mom was seen by the neuro-opthamologist in Columbia, South Carolina. She said that Mom's left eye was damaged and couldn't be restored. There was no damage to the retina in the right eye, and she could regain some sight in that eye. There was a spot in the right eye that she could see through, but she must be trained how to find it. The spot was right next to her nose. This doctor felt that Mom's sight would not get any worse. She referred Mom for two MRIs at McLeod Hospital on March 20 at 1:45 P.M. She also wanted to see Mom again after the MRI on April 1 at 2:00 P.M.

March 19, 2009

Stacy, Tracy, and I cleaned out Mom's house today. I called Jenny, my mother's case manager, regarding getting a home health aide for Mom. She said she would mail some forms for me to sign and return to her.

March 20, 2009

Mom moved in with us today. I had her room all ready and hoped she would be happy with us. Stacy and Tracy brought Mom and her belongings to the house in the early afternoon. When Mom got to the house, she said to me, "Well, here I am." This would be a big change for Mom as well as for me. Although I was retired, I now had a full-time job. I told Mom that we wanted her there, and we would do whatever is necessary to make her feel at home. Mom started feeling at home right away and told me that she wanted to be there. She further stated "I love my son, and I know he wanted me to stay with him, but he won't be able to take care of my personal needs like another woman can." We all knew that Mom was old fashioned and would never want any man bathing her—not even her son. Tracy later told me that she didn't think I could take care of Mom with my bad back. I must admit that I thought the same way at first. But I remembered very quickly that I could do anything with the help of God.

Stacy and Tracy went back to Chesterfield to finish cleaning out Mom's house. The first thing I did was to make sure Mom was comfortable. I unpacked all her clothes and put them away. Mom said she loved her room. I had already hung some of her pictures and had her personal things on the dresser. The room looked like she was still in her room in Chesterfield. She loved everything. I could only sit and talk with Mom for a little while because she had an appointment that afternoon. We got ready, and I took her to McLeod Hospital for two MRIs. We returned home, and she settled down at the house. Since she had to come out of her room to go to the bathroom, I put the portable pot in her room at night. This would be a challenge for me because I know she would rather be at

Samuel's house. However, she was determined to make the best of it and so was I.

March 21, 2009

When Mom got up, I made her breakfast and cleaned her room. Mom sat in the sunroom and ate her breakfast. She loved sitting by the window looking out. I didn't really know how much she was able to see, but she seemed to know what was going on.

Some of my cousins from Charlotte came to see Mom today. Mom enjoyed having company but got very tired after a while. George and I rarely had company in Connecticut, and this was the first company we had since Mom moved in with us in South Carolina. Stacy, Tracy, and Carnel [Stacy's friend] were also at the house. After a few hours, Mom said she was tired and went to bed. We all sat and talked until they left. I cleaned up and went to bed myself, as I was also exhausted.

March 23, 2009

I was scheduled to see my back doctor today, but I forgot about my appointment. I checked the calendar, and it was written as plain as day, but it just slipped my mind. The only thing I can say is that I had a lot going on. Keeping track of appointments for three people can be difficult at times, but I thank God I never missed one of Mom's medical exams. Tracy and Stacy left South Carolina today and returned to their respective homes.

March 27, 2009

Mom complained about having a sharp pain in her left eye. She also said that her left eye itched. I contacted the doctor and was told that it is normal for the eye to itch. However, the eye specialist would check her eye out when she goes for her appointment in a few days.

Chapter 7

***

In Search of Services

One morning I woke up and sat on the side of my bed. My head was spinning, and I could see my life passing right before my eyes. My mind was racing as though I was having a nervous breakdown. I thought, *"What is wrong with me?"* In the last few months, my life had changed drastically, but I still had much more to do to get things established for Mom. Yes, I was exhausted, and my entire being was feeling the strain from it all, but I knew I could do all things through Christ who strengthens me. I knelt and prayed, and asked the Lord for strength. **"My soul melteth for heaviness: strengthen thou me according unto thy word" (Psalm 119:28).**

I had been working hard to find services for Mom. I was able to find an excellent medical provider, but she was still in need of a foot doctor. I was also working on finding some in-home services through her current case manager. When Mom moved in with me, she lost all of the services she had in Chesterfield. Now it was up to me to get those services reactivated. Some may ask since she was being cared for by me full time, why would I need services for her? My answer would be, "Try walking a week in my shoes and then ask me why." First of all, my mother was entitled to those services. Furthermore, anyone taking on the responsibility of caring for a loved one needs support and any kind of help available. Even though she was living with me, some in-home services would still be beneficial to her as well as me. Yes, I admitted I needed help, but where do I start?

Researching various services for the elderly, I was not in my comfort zone because my prior experience was focused on the younger generation. Not only was I not familiar, but I was also residing in a totally different state. Yes, I was completely lost. I was in need of services for an elderly lady with limited income.

I started in the Yellow Pages to see what elderly services were available. I was able to locate a number of service providers with services that would be beneficial for my mother, which included:

Access services, such as information and referral, outreach, case management, escort, and transportation.

In-home services, which include chore, homemaker, personal care, home-delivered meals, and home repair and rehabilitation.

Community services, including senior center, congregate meal, day care, nursing home ombudsman, elder abuse prevention, legal, employment counseling and referral, health promotion, and fitness programs.

Caregiver services, such as respite, counseling, and education programs.

Since I had only recently returned to South Carolina, I was unsure which of these services were available here. I also thought, *"Are these services free?"* One of our major concerns was how were we going to finance these services, whether in the home or in a facility. My mother was on Medicare, but I quickly learned that Medicare was limited and would not cover a lot of services. I also learned that some of the services Mom needed were not covered by her particular insurance carrier; the bulk of these in-home services had to be paid out of pocket. I had my work cut out for me.

I got on the Internet and started searching for services. According to the statistics, 80 percent of the care provided to the elderly in this country was provided by family members. I admit that it was a challenge exploring all the community-based services. It was difficult at first, as people would keep transferring you from place to place before you reach the correct department. Dealing with social service agencies can be challenging. They wanted to know what kind of help or services I needed without explaining what the services were. I spoke with some very nice and some not so nice people. Although there were well-trained and well-versed professionals in the aging services community, reaching someone willing to help consumers through the process was an extremely disheartening quest.

I didn't know if my mother was eligible for any of these services. However, when I talked to Samuel about it, he said, "If anyone is eligible, Mom should be." My mother was now eighty-six years old, and she was still in her right mind. She had no signs of dementia, which was a blessing. She loved having people around her because she lived most of her life in a family setting until her children left home. She had been doing okay in her home until she went blind, but now she needed someone to take care of her full time.

If you are heavily burdened with care obligations right now and desperate for solutions to dilemmas, remember that there is hope. There are agencies that can help you but finding them can be a challenge. Available services are not always advertised. There are people trained to assist with parental care. There are also agencies who receive federal funding to aid the elderly, but you have to search for these services. Believe me, if you have older parents who may need your support one day, start now. Do not wait for it to hit you in the face. In my research, I learned that there were more than nine million Americans over the age of sixty-five who lived alone. Many of these individuals had no one to turn to if they needed help. Lack of a caregiver is a serious problem for those older persons who have chronic conditions and limitations in their ability to care for themselves and their homes. Their problems are often compounded by increased medical costs due to poor health and the need for more supportive services.

I also learned that the Older Americans Act of 1965 as amended called for a range of programs that offered services and opportunities for older Americans, especially those at risk of losing their independence. I called Mom's case manager and signed her up for Life Line before she left her home. I also signed her up for Meals on Wheels and companion hours. This was a start and also a big help.

Now that Mom was living with me in Florence, I needed to request services for this area. I called Mom's case manager again about transferring services to Florence County. I told her that I never received the paperwork. She said she would send the paperwork out again. Once I completed the paperwork and sent it back, she would go from there.

Chapter 8

***

Mom Saw Daylight

> "If my people, which are called by my name, shall humble themselves, and pray, and seek my face, and turn from their wicked ways; then will I hear from heaven, and will forgive their sin, and will heal their land." —2 Chronicles 7:14

April 1, 2009

Samuel and I took Mom to the neuro-eye specialist in Columbia, South Carolina, today. Mom complained about not being able to distinguish night from day. We told the doctor about the sharp pain in her left eye and that it itches. The specialist said that the MRIs looked good and were normal for her age. There was a blood flow problem to the optic nerve in both eyes, but the left eye was worse. The blood work was also good. The specialist thought it was okay to remove the cataract but said Mom still might not be able to see. The eye doctors could look behind the cataract to see if there was a possibility of her seeing after it was removed. If so, it could be removed. If not, there was no need to go through the surgery. She recommended the Commission for the Blind, a low-vision service to help Mom to learn to live with her sight loss.

April 2, 2009

This morning Mom got up as usual and came out of her room for breakfast. As she sat in her chair, she looked out of the window and said, "Is something shining outside?" I moved the curtain and saw that the sun was shining on the house next door. I told Mom that it was the sun. Mom said, "I knew I saw a light." Later we went outside and sat under the carport. All of a sudden, Mom shouted, "Dollie, it's day. I can see day." I asked her to explain exactly what she was seeing. Mom said that since she went blind, she could not distinguish night from day. When she went to bed, it was night. When she got up in the morning, it was night. She could see shadows out of her right eye, but they appeared dark and blurry. She was able to find her way around the house, but everything and every day was in darkness. Mom had not seen daylight since she went blind the beginning of March 2009. But I thank God for all His many blessings, as Mom saw daylight today for the first time since she went blind. That was definitely a blessing.

I called Mom's case manager again regarding in-home services for Mom. Mom had been totally without services since she left Chesterfield in February 2009 and came to live with me. A home health aide for Mom would have been very helpful during this time because she was partially blind and could not be by herself. We made sure Mom was never left alone. Samuel called often to see if we needed anything or if we needed to go anywhere. One Sunday, Samuel showed up at my door and said, "I'm here to stay with Mom, so that you can go to church." It was hard in the beginning because the life that I knew before no longer existed. I couldn't go to church on Sundays like I did before or go out to dinner after church or do anything at the spur of the moment. I had to make sure someone was in the house all the time. Mom's case manager called me about Angelic Home Care, and said she would call to see if they had any openings and if they did, when they could start. I reminded the case manager that Mom was entitled to these services, and I needed help. She said she would check into it right away.

April 3, 2009

The second day of daylight felt good to my mother. We sat outside almost all day. It was like she was seeing God's beautiful earth for the first time. She said, "The sun is shining, and I can see it." She looked at the birds, trees, grass, and even the bugs crawling on the ground. Every time a car passed during the day, she would look until they drove out of sight. At one time she said, "I can see all the way up yonder," pointing to a distant church at the end of the road. All of a sudden, Mom looked at me and said, "Dollie, I saw day two days now." I answered and said, "Yes, Mom, you sure did. I believe God is going to restore your sight." She said, "I do, too."

When I thought about my mother losing her sight at the age of eighty-six, I thought about how so many people took life, health, and strength for granted. I remembered how my mother had to feel the plate to find her food. This was so sad to me. She would drop food all over her clothes and floor without knowing it. She had to feel the walls to find her way to the bathroom. We had to dress her and lead her around the house. Although she tried to do things for herself, someone had to be there all the time to make sure she didn't bump into anything. We had to leave the lights on all the time because she said it was too dark. The neurological specialist said Mom might regain some of her sight in her right eye but not to the point of where she was before. The test showed she had a spot that was good, but Mom had to be trained how to find that spot. They recommended services for the blind.

Mom was never trained, but somehow she was able to find the spot on her own. At first, she would keep turning her head until she found the spot, but everyday it got easier. Yes, she is still blind in her left eye, but some vision in one eye is better than none. Mom said, "I can't see well, but I can see well enough to get around and distinguish night from day." Mom was so thankful that she could see enough to do things for herself. When some of Mom's sight returned in her right eye, she was up early every morning and would sit outside all day. At times her clothes didn't match, but that didn't matter because we were home. We even ate outside with the gnats and all. Mom and I talked about everything during that time. She provided lots of family history for my first book. I kept picking her brain, and she loved it. Every time I wrote something, she asked me to read it to her, and I did. She would listen to me reading my notes, and soon she would ask to hear what I had written about a particular medical appointment. Mom kept telling me that I should let her friends and family read my notes so they would know what she was going through. I believe she enjoyed it as much as I did. She also loved sitting in the sunroom and under the carport watching the cars go by. She told me *"I'm going to miss this sunroom and carport when we move."*

April 4, 2009

My mother and I sat outside again today and talked about different things. It was such a beautiful day. The sun was shining, and there was a slight breeze in the air. My mother was so thankful that God restored some of her sight. My mother talked about going to church when she got rid of the cough. My mother also talked about how she laid in bed one night at my brother's house and cried. She prayed that her children wouldn't put her in a nursing home. Her stepmother, Miss Bell, told her that she was going to sign herself into a nursing home because her children didn't care about her. Mom said when she told her that she was going to live with me, Miss Bell cried. I told my mother that this is her home; she doesn't live with me—we live together. This made her happy, and she smiled.

April 6, 2009

Mom had an appointment with ENT in Hartsville because of her chronic cough. The doctor said that since Mom had not responded to any of the prescribed medications, it led him to believe that something else was causing the cough. She had post persistent nasal drainage. He suggested stopping the Lotrel for two months, as ACE inhibitors and ACE receptor blockers can sometimes cause coughs. He recommended having her primary physician switch Lotrel for something else for two months. He further stated that her food could be going down the wrong way. He wanted a CAT scan of her chest with contrast and also a modified barium swallow with esophagram at McLeod Hospital. He wanted the CAT scan and swallow test results sent to him with the reports. Mom was scheduled to see the ENT doctor again in four weeks. Her next appointment was on May 1 at 11:10 A.M.

April 6, 2009

I called Mom's primary physician regarding changing Lotrel as her ENT doctor had suggested.

April 8, 2009

Mom's doctor called in new medication into Walgreens. He replaced Lotrel with Benicar. I went and picked the new medicine up.

April 9, 2009

I took Mom to McLeod Outpatient Clinic for her CAT scan, swallow test, and lab work. I completed forms with background information on Mom. I also stopped by the X-ray file room to pick up the film for Mom's ENT doctor. Mom looked good for her appointment. I teased her and asked if she was meeting someone at the hospital that I didn't know about. She laughed and said, "Dollie, stop your foolishness."

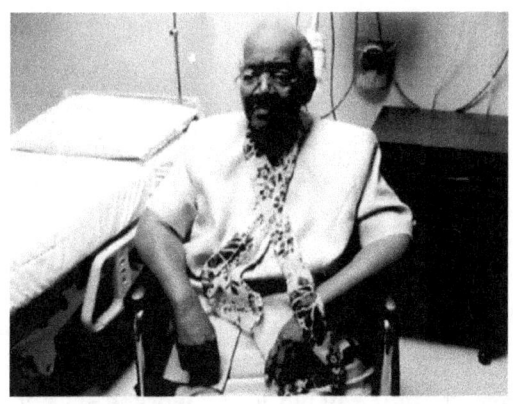

Mom at McLeod Medical Center

Story of Mr. Johnson

While at McLeod Hospital on April 9 with Mom, a lady sitting next to me in the waiting room started a conversation with me. She first asked if I was with my mother, and I said yes. I told her that my mother went blind suddenly and had to be moved out of her house. She was now staying with me. She told me that she took care of her father for two years before he died. Her father got sick without any warning. His name was Mr. Johnson. She said that she had no sisters or brothers. However, she did have a very supportive cousin who was there for her. When her father first got sick, she was devastated. She didn't know what to do or where to start. She knew she had to work to support herself. The doctor she worked for told her about a nursing home (Faith Nursing Home), and she was able to get him in. He stayed at this nursing for four months until she could get things together and people to help her care for him. After she got everything arranged, she took him out of the nursing home and moved him in with her. She said that everyone told her that she didn't know what she was doing. Once she took him out, it would be impossible to get him back in.

She said that when her father died, he took ten years of her life with him. It was a very draining experience for her. She told me she learned how to cry and call on her Lord. Her father slept all day while she worked. When she got home and finally went to bed, her father was up all night getting into one thing after another. One night she woke up and caught her father taking the box spring mattress outside on the porch. He had already removed the top mattress and was on his way outside with the other. When she saw him, she immediately said, "Daddy, you better take those mattresses back in your room." He looked at her and said, "I can't because I don't have anyone to help me." He was not in his right mind and would tear up her house at night.

One night, he got himself at the bottom of the bed. She got on her knees and pulled him back up. In doing that, she hurt her back. She went back and forth to the back doctor, but was unable to get relief. She finally went through back surgery and had been doing better. She wished me luck and told me not to let this new challenge consume me. She said to ask the Lord for strength and find time for myself.

April 9, 2009

Mom also had an appointment at Carolinas Center for Sight in Florence. They checked Mom's eyes. They said Mom's left eye did not look promising. He wanted his partner to see Mom, as he was the doctor who saw her initially in 2000. I did not know that Mom had been seen there before. I learned that Carolinas Center for Sight removed the cataracts from Mom's right eye in 2000. While we were out, I picked up Mom's medication (Benicar, 20 mg a day) at Walgreens.

When we arrived home, the nurse was there from Angelic Home Health Services. I had been trying for months to get in-home services switched from Chesterfield to Florence. Since Mom moved in with me, she has been without a home health aide. This had been an experience. The nurse checked Mom and took her blood. Her blood pressure was 193/83. I requested a shower extension chair and an extension shower head. The nurse trained me on how to check Mom's sugar. I was told that the home health aide was scheduled to start on April 13. I was happy to get that news.

Dollie's Diary

***

April 10, 2009

Today was my sixty-fourth birthday. I received gifts in the mail from my daughter, Latisha and her family. I also got phone calls from my friends and family.

April 13, 2009

The home health aide started today. I introduced her to Mom and showed her what she had to do. Mom would be getting nineteen hours a week—ten PT hours and nine companion hours. The aide was at the house for five hours today. I stayed around the house to answer questions and to get to know the aide. I would never leave Mom with someone I didn't know anyway. So George or I stayed home with Mom until I felt comfortable enough to leave Mom with the aide.

April 16, 2009

Today I was closing on the new house on Homewood Avenue. Once we closed, I would start working on the house, so that we could move in. In the meantime, we were staying in the old house on Stagecoach Road. It was tight, but we were getting by. The new house was larger and Mom would have her own space. Mom would have the master bedroom, so she would have a bathroom in her room. Once we removed the carpet, installed hardwood floors, and painted, we could move in. The closing went well, and I was given the keys to the house.

I took Mom to the attorney's office to sign the power of attorney papers I had drawn up. It was getting more and more difficult for Mom to sign permission statements when I took her to the hospital. At times, they would not allow me to sign for her, and she would struggle signing all the forms. They said the only way I could sign for her was to have power of attorney. Today, Mom signed the forms that would be filed in court.

April 17, 2009

Mom and I went for a ride today. When Mom was feeling well, we took many rides around Florence and the surrounding areas. She loved looking at the big houses and office buildings. She would always say, "I love Florence." I took her to get something to eat and to see the new house. She loved the new house, especially the big brick chimney. She said, "You don't have to paint my room because I love the color." Mom seemed so excited about the house and said she couldn't wait to move.

April 18, 2009

I called Tracy last night and asked if she could come and help with Mom while I did some work at the new house. Tracy said she was not able to come at that time. Since Tracy was not available, I called my son, JR, in Charlotte and asked if he would help me out for a week. Since he was trying to get back to Connecticut, he said he would help out if I helped him get to Connecticut. I agreed and told him I would pick him up early the next morning.

April 19, 2009

I got up early this morning and drove to Charlotte to pick JR up. It was a good ride. He was ready when I got there. We drove back to Florence. The entire trip took me a little over six hours.

April 20, 2009

Mom had an appointment with her new primary physician, Dr. Baker. It took me hours on the phone to locate a doctor in Florence willing to take Mom's insurance. She was finally accepted by First Choice. Mom loved this new doctor. He took Mom's hat off her head and wore it during the entire examination. Mom loved that. He was so personable. Mom weighed 181 pounds. Her blood pressure was 193/83. She was given a new prescription (Norvasc, 10 mg/day). I filled the prescription at Walgreens before going home.

April 24, 2009

The house in Connecticut finally sold. This was the second closing for me this month. The house had been on the market for over two years, with one thing happening after another. We had to go to Connecticut twice because of that house. I sacrificed a lot to relocate to South Carolina in order to help take care of Mom before selling my house in Connecticut. I had many offers, but most of them fell through. I took a big loss, but I thanked God that chapter of my life was finally closed. I did all the paperwork electronically with the help of my attorney. I received a telephone call from the attorney's office this afternoon stating that the closing went well. I now had closure in Connecticut.

April 26, 2009

George

George fell this morning at the Homewood Avenue address and got a deep cut in his shoulder. When he got to the house, JR said that he had a deep cut that needed stitches. I looked at the cut, and it did appear deep. I immediately took him to Carolina Hospital. JR stayed with Mom. George got ten stitches. While in the emergency room, the doctor noticed that his heart rate was slow (thirty-five to forty-six beats per minute). He said the low heart rate might have caused him to fall. They sent George for a number of tests (i.e., blood work, X-rays, EKG, blood pressure, etc.). They wanted to hospitalize him for a few days to monitor his heart rate. They also gave him a tetanus shot. They started an IV line and admitted him. George was not pleased about being hospitalized.

JR was scheduled to take the train to Connecticut tonight at 11:00 P.M. I thought, *"What am I going to do now? I still had so much to do at the old house and the new house."* I had to finish packing to move, paint the new house, take care of Mom, and George was in the hospital. I needed some help. That night I took JR to the train station, and he went back to Connecticut. He was willing to stay, but we were unable to change the tickets. I was so stressed because I didn't know anyone in Florence to call for help. Who would I get to stay with Mom? Samuel was willing to come, but he was sick. I knew Stacy would come in a heartbeat, but she and Gloria were in Connecticut working. The only other person to call was Tracy. I called Tracy to see if she could come for a few days. When she said she was not able to come, I broke down and started crying. I had no other options. When I told her that George was in the hospital, and I needed someone to stay with Mom, she immediately said she would be there the next day. I told her if she would come and stay with Mom until George was out of the hospital, I would pay for the trip.

<u>April 27, 2009</u>

George's heart rate was still slow. The staff doctor came in and said George needed a pacemaker. We signed all the necessary paperwork, as the procedure was scheduled for 2:00 P.M. He received a dual-chamber pacemaker. The doctor said everything went well.

This afternoon I received an application in the mail from the South Carolina Commission for the Blind for Mom to receive services through the Independent Living Program for the elderly blind. I wasn't sure if these services were appropriate for Mom now that she was residing with me. I tried to contact them regarding their services but was unable to connect.

<u>April 28, 2009</u>

Mom had an appointment with Carolinas Center for Sight. The physician said that her left eye was gone. He felt that there was no need to remove the cataracts. He said the right eye could be better if the inflammation was treated. He had not received the reports from the specialist. Mom had seen the specialist on March 17 and April 1, but no reports had been received.

April 29, 2009

George was discharged from the hospital this afternoon. The doctor told him to keep his arm immobilized for forty-eight hours. He also needed to keep the pacemaker incision dry for one week. George did nothing the doctor told him to do. He was not a good patient. He took the sling off his arm as soon as he walked in the house. When I tried to remind him of the discharge instructions, he got angry and said that it was uncomfortable. He refused to put the sling back on.

Tracy returned to North Carolina this morning. She was such a big help to me, as she stayed with Mom and totally took care of her while I was either at the hospital or the new house working. It was worth paying for the trip. I was glad George was finally out of the hospital because now I could focus on completing the new house, so that we could move in. Mom was upset when Tracy left, as she felt she should have stayed longer to help me. I told Mom that Tracy did help me, and I appreciated what she did.

May 1, 2009

I took Mom to see ENT specialist in Hartsville regarding her cough. The cough seemed to be getting worse. The doctor reviewed the results of the swallow test from April 9. Mom was told to put her chin to her chest when she swallowed liquid. He also wanted Mom to eat at the table, sitting straight in her chair. He did not want Mom watching TV when she ate because there should be absolutely no distractions. The CAT scan looked good. Mom had two or three small cysts in her kidney on the right side. She also had some inflammation and swelling in her left sinus. He wanted Mom to stop taking her Benicar (ACE inhibitor) for one month to see if that would help her cough. Mom was given a shot for her congestion.

I called Mom's primary physician's office regarding stopping Mom's Benicar. The nurse practitioner said she spoke with Dr. Baker, and he did not want to change Mom's Benicar. He changed Mom's Norvasc to Topral (Metroprolol Tartrate, 50 mg). He did not believe that the Benicar was causing Mom's cough.

Sunday, May 3, 2009

I went to church for the first time since March 1. It felt so good being in church again. Since Mom had been with me, it had been difficult for me to leave the house, especially on Sundays. First of all, it took months to get in-home services in Florence. After the services started, it took time finding a stable person to come. We went through numerous home health aides but finally found an excellent young lady that Mom liked. Mom seemed to be doing much better every day.

May 4, 2009

I took George for his follow-up appointment at Advanced Cardiology Associates to check the pacemaker. There was some minor discharge but no need for alarm. The bandage was removed. George's blood pressure was 122/80. His heart rate was sixty-two.

May 11, 2009

My back was still giving me a lot of problems. I tried not to let Mom know how bad my back was hurting because she would worry. I took pain medication but not as much as the doctor prescribed because I did not want to become addicted. I suffered through most of the pain. Today I had an appointment with my back doctor. He gave me a local injection in the lump while in his office. He also gave me a back brace and suggested physical therapy.

May 12, 2009–May 14, 2009

I had been working on the new house for a month, and we were now ready for the move. It took a while to complete the work that was needed, and there was still more to do, but we could do the remainder while in the house. I worked at the new house during the day and packed up the old house at night. On the home health aide's short days, Mom would come to the new house with me and sit outside under the carport while I worked. I also cooked every night so that Mom would have a good meal every day. Yes, I was exhausted. I painted three of the four bedrooms. Mom did not want me to paint her room because she liked the green color already on the walls. I had all the carpet removed and replaced with hardwood floors. The contractor sanded and stained all the floors throughout the house, so they would match; they looked like they were new. I had been taking boxes over to the house for over a week and storing them in the workshop or the den. The boxes were everywhere at both houses. We were all ready for the move, which was scheduled for tomorrow. Now I must say good-bye to the little house in the country. Mom and I would truly miss the sunroom.

May 15, 2009

Today was the big day. We were all moving into the new house. I packed a bag for each of us with all our personal items and put them in my car early this morning. Mom's home health aide was at the house for five hours today and that was a big help. The movers came early and started loading the trucks. It took all day to move, but by sundown, everything was at the new address on Homewood Avenue.

May 19, 2009

I took Mom to see Dr. Baker this morning. She weighed 184 pounds. Her blood pressure was really high (209/74). Dr. Baker was very concerned about Mom's blood pressure. He reviewed her chart and checked her vital signs. Mom's meds were changed. He said she should not take any aspirin while her blood pressure is high. He increased her Benicar and Topral. She will continue with Singulair, Vesicare, and the Nasonex nose spray. He gave Mom a new prescription for Benicar and Topral, and increased Mom's dosage. He added a water pill to reduce pressure. He wanted to see Mom the following week. He asked me to check Mom's blood pressure two times a day. Mom told the doctor that she was almost constipated. He did not want to prescribe a laxative. He told Mom to drink a lot of water and eat fruit and fiber. I told Dr. Baker that Mom had a colonoscopy on 9/25/08, and she had no blockage at that time. I let him know that it was recommended that she have a colonoscopy every year. I also reminded Dr. Baker about Mom's cough. He said he was not too concerned about the cough or colonoscopy at that time because if he was unable to get her blood pressure down, she won't be here to do anything. He was more concerned about Mom possibly having another stroke. Dr. Baker gave me his cell phone number and said to call if there were any changes.

I started taking Mom's blood pressure two, three, and sometimes four times a day. Her blood pressure would go up and down daily. I have always kept notes on Mom regarding her medicine and appointments, but after this point, I became even more diligent about keeping record of her condition.

May 21, 2009–May 22, 2009

For the last two mornings, Mom was up, dressed, and sitting on the back porch before 7:30 A.M. I walked outside and asked her how she was doing, and she said, "I feel fine. I am enjoying the sunshine and looking at your beautiful pool." I checked Mom's blood pressure, and it stayed between 178/80 to 180/78. Mom was full of energy, and looked rested and in high spirits. After she ate breakfast, the home health aide took her for a short walk. Mom sat outside almost all afternoon. Samuel stopped by, and she was happy to see him. I was glad Mom was doing so well.

May 23, 2009

Mom's blood pressure was 226/87 to 236/88 this morning. I called Dr. Baker regarding her high blood pressure. He told me to increase her water pill and give Mom her evening dose of Metopralol immediately. I checked Mom's blood pressure four more times this date. At 11:26 A.M. it was 192/75, twice at 2:35 P.M., 196/71 & 222/82 and at 2:55 P.M., 203/75. I called Dr. Baker back. He said her blood pressure was still too high. He told me to restart the Norvasc (10 mg/day) immediately. Although her blood pressure was elevated, Mom said she felt good. I made her a good dinner, and she ate very well.

May 24, 2009

Mom's blood pressure was better today. I checked it three times, and the readings were lower: 182/63, 175/73, and 163/61. Mom had a very good day.

George was taken to Carolinas Hospital Emergency Room this afternoon for a swollen foot. He dropped the lawn mower on it three days ago. His left leg was also swollen. They did X-rays on both feet, and there were no broken bones. We were at the hospital over six hours. I was so worried because Mom was home alone. I couldn't call to check on her because she never answered the phone. So I left George in the emergency room and ran home to check on Mom. Mom was in bed asleep when I arrived.

I went back to the hospital and waited with George until he was released. He was given medication for his feet and for the pain.

Today was Clarence Jr's birthday and with all that was going on, I almost forgot to call and wish him a Happy Birthday. When I got home, I called Clarence Jr. and our daughter Latisha to let them know about George's condition. Latisha said that he might need a total physical workup. His balance had been off for months, and he was beginning to have difficulty in other areas as well. I called his doctor and requested an appointment for him to have a complete physical.

May 25, 2009

Mom did well today. She was in a good mood and talked a lot about Grove Baptist Church. After breakfast, she sat outside for a long time. We watched the cars go by and walked around the yard. She loved the big chimney on the house and always talked about how big the house was. I made one of her favorite meals (corn soup), and she loved it. She always told me that no one could make soup like me. When she finished her meal, she said, "Dollie, I enjoyed my dinner." Her blood pressure was still down at 182/77 and 159/68. After dinner, she watched some of her shows and retired for the night.

May 26, 2009

Mom had an appointment with Dr. Baker today. She got up early and ate her breakfast. We had to wait before she was seen, and Mom is not a patient person. When they called her, they checked her vital signs and weight. She weighed 184 pounds. Her blood pressure was 153/76, and her heart rate was fifty-four. The appointment went well. Mom was in a good mood, and she looked good today. She and Dr. Baker got along very well. After leaving First Choice, we stopped to get something to eat. After we got home, she sat outside for a while.

May 27, 2009–June 4, 2009

Every morning I would go into Mom's room and ask her how she was doing. She kept telling me this week, "I feel fine. I am not in any pain." She would come to the table every morning for breakfast, and her appetite was very good. She would eat breakfast, lunch, and dinner during the day and have her snacks at night. I tried to keep healthy snacks in the house for her. She told me she got hungry at night, so I always put something in her room for her to snack on when she got hungry. Mom even started taking short walks with the home health aide. She would sit outside under the carport and watch the traffic. I continued to check her blood pressure and sugar daily, keeping a record of both for the doctor. I informed him when they were elevated. This week, her pressure was up and down. It ran from 147/67 to 217/74. Her blood sugar was also up and down. It ran from 116 to 201. Nevertheless, Mom was in good spirits and showed no signs of feeling bad in any way. This was a good week for her physically. She called Miss Bell and her best friend, Mary Burk this week and told them both how happy she was. I believed Mom was happy because she said it often. Before she went to bed, we sat and talked for a while. Mom told me, "Dollie, I will never forget what you and George did for me." I told Mom "What I do for you, I want to do. We want you here. This is your home." She smiled and went to bed. When I checked on her later, she was eating her snacks.

June 5, 2009-June 6, 2009

Mom was doing well this morning. Her blood pressure was down, running from 161/76 to 186/67 today. She was full of energy and was up early, dressed, and sitting on the back porch when I got up. Yes, today started off pretty good. I, too, woke up with a burst of energy and decided to stop procrastinating about cleaning the old house. I got dressed and told George that we should go over to the house on Stagecoach Road and pick up the remainder of the items for the yard sale, which was to be held the next day. It was a good day to get it done because the home health aide would be at the house with Mom for five hours today.

After we cleaned the old house and got back home, Mom happily told me that she walked today. Not just a short walk, mind you—she went to the end of the street and back. That was absolutely too far for her to walk after the two weeks that she had. The home health aide chimed in and said that my mother had to stop three times to rest before she got back to the house. Mom was so exhausted by the time she reached the house that she had to sit outside and rest again before she could enter the house. This was absolutely too much. I asked the home health aide, "Didn't you think to turn around when she got tired the first time?" She said Mom wanted to go all the way to the end of the street. I reminded Mom of what her doctor said about not overdoing it. He specifically told Mom that she should start doing things gradually. Mom never listened to the doctor or me. Whenever she felt good, she thought she could do whatever came to mind. I was very upset with Mom and the home health aide. I told Mom that I needed to be able to trust her when I was not around. Mom promised not to do it again. Mom was so tired, that she would have promised me anything to get me out of her room.

Mom rested most of the day. I fixed her a good healthy dinner, and she ate the entire meal. We sat and talked for about an hour until I got ready to take a swim. Mom wanted to put her feet in the water, which was fine with me. I put on my bathing suit and helped her outside to the pool. When she put her feet in the water, she was very happy and said it felt good. She kept her feet in the water for about twenty good minutes while watching me swim. I helped her out of the pool and back into the house. I made sure she was in bed before I undressed and got ready for bed myself. About an hour later, I heard my mother call me. When I got to the room, she said, "Dollie, I'm sick. I need one of my pain pills." I asked what was wrong, and she said she hurt all over. I immediately gave her the pain pill, but it did not work. She tossed and turned, but felt no relief.

I eventually had to get her dressed and take her to McLeod Hospital Emergency Room. She told the doctors that she had severe stomach pain and that her entire body ached all over. We were there all night. My mother was not a patient woman, especially when she went to the doctor or the hospital. She constantly complained about everything. I called my brother around 3:00 A.M. and asked him to relieve me, as my garage sale was in a few hours, and I needed to set things out. Samuel and his girlfriend Marie arrived around 5:00 A.M. I went home and started putting things out for my garage sale. My mother was sent home around 11:00 A.M. Although the doctors did not find anything wrong with her, she was given antibiotics for five days and some more pain pills. They told Mom to follow up with her primary care provider and take the medication as prescribed. Mom was extremely weak and stayed in the house the remainder of the day. Mom was very tired after being up all night, but I had people coming all day for the garage sale. Samuel stayed and helped with Mom.

He made her something to eat and put her to bed. After the garage sale, I put the items that didn't sell away and went to bed myself. I was totally exhausted. I believe both Mom and I slept all night.

June 7, 2009–June 30, 2009

Mom was okay the rest of the month. She kept saying, "I don't feel bad. I'm just a little weak." Her blood pressure had been much better lately and was running between 125/57 to 156/66. It only went up to 191/83 once and dropped back down. Mom continued to sit outside and watch the cars go by almost every day. I believe she learned her lesson about walking so far because she was now only walking around the yard and to the mailbox. She blamed sticking her feet in the pool for her latest hospital episode. She said, "That water made me sick." Yes, the chemicals could have caused some type of reaction, but I also reminded her that it could have been her taking that long walk. The doctor told Mom to take it easy, but Mom tried to walk a mile. I had been trying to stay close because I didn't really trust her right now. Unfortunately, I missed my back appointment on June 8, but I did go for my echocardiogram on June 10. I could only blame myself for missing my own appointments. If I could keep track of Mom and George's appointments, I should have been able to keep track of mine. It was important for me to take care of myself because if something happened to me, who would take care of them?

June 11, 2009

I had been trying to keep up with everything for Mom and George, but it was becoming more and more difficult. I woke up at 2:00 A.M. with a severe headache. My head felt like it was going to burst. I was in so much pain that I thought I was going to have a stroke. I anointed my head and prayed for healing. I got some relief, but the pain was still there. These headaches had been more frequent, but this one was scary. I was really stressed out about George, as this was not a good month for him.

June 15, 2009–June 24, 2009

George's health seemed to be steadily failing. This was a bad time for him. I was going crazy trying to keep George safe and take care of Mom. This week George was hurting so badly that he was unable to stand on his left leg. One night he tried using Mom's walker, but that was a total disaster. His balance was so off that it made it worse. One night, he fell in the bathroom, and I tried to get in to help him, but the door was locked. He stayed on the floor for a long time. I kept asking if he was all right, and he said he was. I offered to call 911, but he did not want me to call. After a while, he was able to get up and open the door. He went back to bed and rested the rest of the night.

The next day, he was worse. He said he had pain going down his left leg. It was so bad that he could hardly walk. He was in bed almost all day. He could hardly go to the bathroom. It was difficult seeing him like that. It was so bad that I told him that I was taking him to the hospital. I called Samuel and asked him to stay with Mom while I took George to the doctor. He said he would. I got George dressed and waited for Samuel to come. When Samuel arrived, George made his way outside to go to the doctor. As soon as Mom saw him in that condition, she was extremely upset. She kept saying, "Y'all help him. You see he's hurting. Help him." It took Samuel and me a few minutes just to get him in the car, but we finally did. It was awful, as George could hardly walk. I drove George to Carolina Hospital, and ran in and got a wheelchair. I helped him out and parked the car. The doctor checked George, and he decided to admit him for tests. George was hospitalized on June 17 and remained in the hospital for a week. He was discharged on June 24, with several medications and clear instructions. Of course he did not follow them. George also blamed the chemicals in the pool water for this hospital episode. George never went back into the pool. In fact, he never went swimming again.

June 25, 2009

Stacy and Tracy came home for a few weeks this month. They took Mom to Samuel's house to spend some time with her. My daughter Latisha and her family also came home for the weekend. Mom stayed with Stacy and Tracy for a few days until my daughter and her family left. I was glad Mom went to Samuel's house because it was hard for her to see George in his condition. She was so worried about him and wanted to help in any way she could. Whenever she saw him stumble, she either jumped or reached out in an effort to help him. This just made him even angrier because he felt that he was fine, and we were exaggerating the problem. We did not know what to do, so we merely tried to stay out of his way.

Although my daughter's visit was brief, I was glad they were there during that particular weekend. My oldest grandson, Robert, wasn't able to come because of school. However, he did call to let us know that Michael Jackson died that morning. George had only been out of the hospital one day, and he was still having a difficult time. For one thing, he kept falling. One morning we heard a loud noise in the den. When we got there, George was on the floor. He later fell in the dining room, and my son-in-law, Calvin, helped him up. He cut his finger, and we had to put a bandage on it. He kept doing careless things such as walking around the pool when he was so unsteady on his feet. It would be one thing if he could swim, but he couldn't, and it was dangerous. Every time he went through the gate, we told my grandson Corey, "Go get your grandfather. He's out there at the pool again." Corey looked out and saw him and said, "Oh man," and went out there to get him. We went through this the entire weekend.

Stacy and Tracy took Mom to see Ms. Bell in Chesterfield. They stopped by the house on the way. Later we all sat outside and had a good time. I was finally able to take some pictures of the four generations with mom, my daughter, Latisha, my granddaughter Tapanga, and myself. Mom seemed to really enjoy herself.

Four Generations: Mom, Dollie, Latisha, and Tapanga

June 27, 2009

My daughter and her family returned to Connecticut. Stacy and Tracy brought Mom home. George was better today. He did not remember anything at all about the weekend. He did not believe he fell or that he got hurt. He asked why he was wearing a bandage.

July 9, 2009

I took Mom for her medical appointment at First Choice. Bad news: I learned Dr. Baker was retiring. Mom loved Dr. Baker and now she had a new doctor, Dr. Shaw. I thought to myself, *"How was this going to work with this new doctor?"* The new doctor impressed Mom right away. Mom weighed 179.5 pounds, her blood pressure was 176/68, and her sugar was 164. He did an X-ray of her chest, which showed her heart was still enlarged. He took blood and urine. He would see her again the beginning of August 2009. After leaving the doctor's office, Mom said, "I love my new doctor."

August 1, 2009–August 27, 2009

Mom had a good month physically. However, her blood pressure and blood sugar were both up and down all month. Her blood pressure went from 138/64 to 208/83. She had an appointment with Dr. Shaw on August 7. He reviewed the daily log of her blood pressure and blood sugar. Mom weighed 176 pounds. Her blood pressure was 141/67 and her sugar was 238 (after eating breakfast).

Gloria, her daughter and grandson came home for a week in August. Gloria brought one of her friends with her. They stayed with Samuel. Mom loved being the center of attention and was a little upset when Gloria spent more time with her friend than with her. One day Mom got up early, got dressed, and went outside immediately after breakfast. She kept asking, "When is Gloria coming?" She sat outside the entire morning. She eventually came in and sat in the den the remainder of the afternoon waiting for them to come. As soon as she went to her room to get ready for bed, they showed up. Mom was so upset. She later said, "Gloria didn't come to see me. If they wanted to spend time with me, they would have come earlier." The next day Gloria came early and spent the whole day with mom. Mom was so happy. Gloria cooked mom some spaghetti, and we all sat outside and enjoyed the day. I also took some pictures.

Mom sitting outside under the carport

Mom's nieces also came from Charlotte to see her during the summer. Mom enjoyed seeing them. We ate, went swimming, and had a good time. One of them braided Mom's hair, but as soon as she left, Mom took it out. When asked why, she said it was so tight that it gave her a headache. I told Mom that she needed to tell people when they were braiding her hair too tight.

<u>August 18, 2009</u>

I took Mom to the Hartsville ENT office today. Mom finally got her hearing aids. Mom was so happy to have those hearing aids; she was hearing sounds that were not even there. On the ride back to the house, Mom told me to call Samuel and Stacy to let them know she was wearing her hearing aids. She said, "You don't have to tell anyone else because no one else cares about what happens to me."

I told Mom that other people care about what happens to her. She said, "Well, they don't think enough about me to call and see how I'm doing. They don't even spend time with me when they come home." Then Mom's voice was soft and almost sad when she said, "Dollie, you know Gloria and Tracy don't think about me? They don't care what happens to me." I was shocked she said that to me. I felt so bad that she felt that way. I stopped the car on the side of the road and said, "Mom, they do love you. Just because they don't call often does not mean they don't care. I continued, "Mom listen to me—all your children love you and care about what happens to you. Don't ever think that we don't care because you are very important to all of us." I thought, *"That's the way Mom must have felt about me when I neglected to call her in the past. I feel so bad. How can I make it up to her?"* Mom was quiet the remainder of our ride home. I hope she heard what I said because we all do love her. I called Stacy and Samuel to let them know Mom had her hearing aids.

Sunday, August 30, 2009

Mom was up early this morning and said she wanted to go to church today. She ate a good breakfast and said she was feeling good. After breakfast she washed up and started getting dressed for church. After I got dressed, I helped her with her hair and finished getting her dressed. She looked really good. George and I took her to Christ

Temple Church in Timmonsville for regular morning worship service. Mom had a good time. She spoke in church, and it was evident that she enjoyed the service very much. She also enjoyed the attention from the pastor and church members. She was the center of attention, as everyone was fussing over her. After church, I fixed her a good dinner, and she ate well. She went to her room, watched Rev. Patterson on TV, and went to bed for the night. I made sure she had ice water in her room and snacks for the night. She rested well all night.

September 8, 2009

I took Mom to see Dr. Shaw this morning. She weighed 183 pounds. Her blood pressure was 185/74. Her sugar was 127. Dr. Shaw changed her medication. He told me to give Mom an extra water pill when her blood pressure was up. He also wanted me to alert him if her blood pressure was over 200 for two consecutive days or more.

After leaving Dr. Shaw's Office, I took Mom to Hartville ENT to see Ms. Wilks. We signed the hearing aid purchase agreement. Ms. Wilks checked Mom's aids to see if they needed any adjustments. Mom was very proud of her hearing aids. However, she did not understand how to put them in or take them out. She was also having problems turning them up and down. I tried to show her how to put them in, but she couldn't grasp it at that time. Hopefully, she would get used to them soon.

September 9, 2009

Mom had been asking to visit Grove Baptist Church one last time. Since she had been doing okay, the idea of her going to church was all right with me. In fact, I agreed to go with her at first. She wanted me to contact Samuel about going the second Sunday, and I did. He said he would go. Mom was pleased about that. Mom had said in the past that she would not go back to her church until she got a new outfit to wear. Mom was extremely proud and somewhat vain. She had always cared about her appearance from as far back as I can remember.

Mom asked me to buy her a new dress, shoes, and a matching hat. I had no problem with that because I was going to buy her a new outfit anyway. While the home health aide was there, I went shopping and bought Mom two outfits: a nice three-piece aqua dress with a matching hat and a two-piece burgundy dress. Mom loved them both. I had her try them on to make sure they fit, and they did. She was a happy woman. Then she asked about the shoes, as she wanted something with a heel. I told Mom that she wasn't getting any high heel shoes because she could fall. Mom had asked Stacy and Tracy to buy her some shoes with a heel in the past, but they also refused to buy them. Mom said that the heels did not have to be high, just a small heel would do. I told Mom that I would take her to the store and let her pick out a nice pair of dress flat shoes. She agreed.

September 10, 2009

Today I took Mom to Shoe Depot to find a pair of flat dress shoes. I asked the lady if I could bring shoes out to my mom to try on, and she agreed. Mom finally picked a pair of shoes she loved, and I went in and bought them. Now, she had her outfit for church.

Then, Mom started talking about what I should wear that Sunday. She said, "Dollie, I want you to wear that purple suit with the matching hat." I was somewhat shocked, but I didn't know why, because that was Mom. Not only did she care about how she looked, she also wanted us to look our best at all times. At first I was a little upset, but I did not want to upset her so I said nothing. Then she said she wanted us to speak, and that was it. I said, "Mom, if the spirit leads me to speak, I will speak. But if it doesn't, I will sit there and say nothing." I thought, *"No, I don't want to disappoint her, but I am not going to Grove Baptist Church."* We grew up in church and, believe me, our parents taught us well. I said, "Mom you have to remember that you and Dad trained us well. We know how to dress and how to speak in public. We will not embarrass you."

Sunday, September 13, 2009

Mom got up early this morning and had her breakfast. After breakfast she started getting ready for church. I helped her get dressed and did her hair. Mom wore her new suit and her new hat with matching jewelry. She put on some lipstick, and she actually looked good. Before leaving for church, Mom's leg gave out on her, and she fell in her bathroom. I actually saw her going down but could not get to her in time. Samuel and I picked her up, and she appeared to be all right. She still wanted to go to church. Samuel and George took Mom to Grove Baptist Church. While in church, Samuel said Mom would not sit still. She was up and down during the entire service. By the time Mom got home, she was so tired that I had to help her undress. She couldn't even come to the table for dinner and had to eat in her room. I checked her blood pressure, and it was up. The remainder of the month was difficult for her, as it took over two weeks for her to regain her strength and get back to normal.

Monday, September 14, 2009

Mom was so tired this morning that she could not even get out of bed. Her blood pressure was so high that I had to call Dr. Shaw. He told me to increase her water pill, which I did. I checked her blood pressure every hour, as it was running 227/95, 183/70, and 220/96. She stayed in bed all day resting.

__Tuesday, September 15, 2009__

Mom was still tired and weak. Her blood pressure was running from 218/80, 205/79, to 176/70. Her blood sugar stayed around 145 and her pulse at fifty-two. I still made her stay quiet and rest. She had absolutely no energy at all.

__Wednesday, September 16, 2009__

Mom was still not doing well. Her blood pressure was running 208/84, 220/97, and 231/87 all day. I was on the phone constantly with Dr. Shaw. He kept giving me instructions regarding her medication. I kept Mom quiet and made her rest all day.

__Thursday, September 17, 2009__

Mom was still visibly tired. This morning she said, "Dollie, I am not well enough to go to church yet. It set me back." I told her to rest and her strength will return. I continued to check her blood pressure every hour. It ran from 220/97, 231/87, and 151/71. Her pulse was from fifty-seven up to sixty-five, blood sugar 146 (fasting).

__Friday, September 18, 2009__

Today Mom was a little better. Her blood pressure stayed around 189/74, pulse was sixty, and her blood sugar was up to 189 (fasting). She still wanted to stay in her room, as she felt weak. I brought her food and stayed close in case she needed me.

Saturday, September 19, 2009

I was surprised she was still tired and weak. Her blood pressure was up again today. It stayed between 201/91 and 209/89, pulse was sixty-one, and blood sugar 129 (fasting). I called the doctor again regarding her pressure. He told me to keep monitoring her pressure and keep him informed. I continued to check her pressure every hour.

Sunday, September 20, 2009

Mom said she felt a little better today. However, her blood pressure was still running high. I kept taking it every hour. I stayed home from church because I was afraid to leave her. I was very concerned. What if she had a stroke? When her blood pressure went up to 231/91, I called Dr. Shaw. He answered his phone while still in church. He told me to give her another dose of her blood pressure medication and take her pressure again. If it failed to go down and if she started showing any signs of unusual behavior, call 911. I gave her another dose of her medication, waited a while, and checked her pressure again. It did go down some.

Monday, September 21, 2009

Mom's blood pressure was 205/86 today. Her blood sugar was 147 and her pulse was fifty-six. I called Dr. Shaw regarding my mother's pressure. He will see her tomorrow.

Tuesday, September 22, 2009

I took Mom to see Dr. Shaw regarding her high blood pressure and elevated sugar that she'd experienced all week. Before going to the doctor, Mom's blood pressure was 206/103, her pulse was sixty-one, and her blood sugar was 140 (fasting). I told him that Mom's fingers are turning blue from being stuck so much to check her blood sugar. He said he wasn't as concerned about her sugar right now. He wanted me to start checking it about three times a week. If I noticed significant changes, I should check it a little more often. If it stayed around the same, I didn't have to stick her as much. He did express some concerns about Mom's cough, as it is back and more severe.

At the doctor's office, she weighed 176.5, which means she lost 6.5 pounds since her last visit. Her blood pressure was 217/85. He said her pulse was too low. He wanted her pulse at seventy beats per minute.

He did an EKG and a chest X-Ray. The X-ray showed that Mom had an enlarged heart. He showed me the X-ray. The heart almost covered her whole chest. The

EKG showed that Mom had an intraventricular block. She could have a heart attack.

Dr. Shaw changed Mom's medication:

- Doubled her Benicar (40 to 80 mg/day) for a short time.
- He added Hydralazine (25 mg 2x/day)
- Replaced Lopressor with Bystolic. Once completed, no more beta blocker.
- He wanted me to call Friday regarding her blood pressure.
- He reminded me that he wanted her pulse at seventy.

Mom had an appointment at ENT in Hartville, but I was afraid to take her because of her high blood pressure. I called and rescheduled. I took Mom home to rest.

September 23, 2009–September 25, 2009

Mom's blood pressure was still high, running 227/112, 211/82, 214/88, and 210/88. Her medication had been changed, but her pressure was still unstable. Mom kept saying, "I should not have gone to church, as it set me back." I told Mom that this could have happened anyway, and we don't really know what brought it on. However, she was convinced that having so many people around her did it. Especially now that Dr. Shaw was saying she should not go to church right now, and she should not be around crowds. Even though the doctor told her this, she still went to church. Mom needed to start listening.

September 25, 2009

I got a call from my daughter, Latisha, regarding my grandbaby. She said she just received the results of Tapanga's EEG. The test revealed benign rolandic epilepsy. However, we were not accepting this diagnosis. God was still in charge.

September 26, 2009–September 29, 2009

Mom's blood pressure was back to normal. Thank you, Jesus. She had more energy and started going back outside to sit under the carport. She now came to the table for her meals. Her appetite was very good, and it appeared she has overcome her tiredness. Mom was back. She had a follow-up appointment with Dr. Shaw on September 29. The appointment went well. She weighed 179 pounds. She had gained 2.5 pounds since her last appointment.

October 1, 2009–October 30, 2009

Mom's blood pressure was up and down this month. It ran from 169/83 to 244/96. Mom seemed to be doing okay physically and said she didn't feel bad. I was just worried about the high blood pressure. I talked with Mom's doctor more than I talked with anyone else. I believe Dr. Mason, Dr. Baker, and Dr. Shaw were all lost when it came to Mom's blood pressure. Was there anyone who could solve this problem?

Mom was into music this month. She listened to the gospel radio stations and played a number of gospel tapes in her room. Stacy brought Mom some tapes when she came home and Mom loved them. The home health aide was coming every day, and it was a big help. Mom was getting nineteen hours a week, which wasn't a lot, but it was better than nothing. Mom was up early every morning for breakfast. Her appetite was still quite good. Although her blood pressure was up and down, she had a lot of energy and seemed to be doing very well the entire month.

On October 1, I had an OB/GYN appointment, and thank God I made it—I have been bad about remembering all of my appointments lately. There were times when I was so busy with Mom and George, that I neglected myself. There were other times when I was just too tired to go and rescheduled the appointment. I knew this was not good, but I felt run down. I was just that exhausted.

October 29, 2009

I took Mom to her medical appointment with Dr. Shaw this morning. He reviewed the log of Mom's blood pressure and blood sugar. He was still concerned about Mom's blood pressure. Mom weighed 175.5 pounds. Her blood pressure was 192/90, and her pulse was sixty-nine. He changed her medication: Hydrahydralazine (three times a day) and Benezar (one a day and an extra pill if her blood pressure goes up). Mom loved her doctor, and he was very good with her.

October 30, 2009

Today was a difficult day, and it was both happy and sad. I finally closed on my parents' house. Yes, the house was sold. I had to be at the Cockrell Law Firm at 159 Main Street in Chesterfield at 9:00 A.M. The closing went well. I never knew that I would feel so many emotions. To begin with, I didn't sleep very well last night; I got up early this morning and was dressed to go to the closing two hours earlier than I needed to be. I waited around the house for a while but finally headed for Chesterfield. I took my time driving, enjoying the scenery. I didn't know when or if I would take that ride from Florence to Chesterfield again. I thought about growing up in that house all the way, sometimes feeling tears of joy and sadness. I had so many mixed feelings. That was home for so many years, and now it would no longer be our family meeting place. I knew within myself that I needed to get rid of the house because I couldn't afford to keep it any longer. We all knew that Mom could no longer live alone. So, knowing all this, why was I having all these feelings? I was truly glad it was finally over.

November 1, 2009–November 31, 2009

This month was a good month for Mom. Even though her blood pressure ran from 196/91 to 242/102, she insisted that she felt as good as I did. I was still worried about her blood pressure, but to my surprise, Mom was full of energy, had a good appetite, and said she never felt better. I was able to spread the home health aide's nineteen hours out so that Mom could have someone on Sunday. I can now go to church, and Mom would not be home alone. Mom was so happy that Stacy gave up a very good job and retired early to help take care of her. Mom told me that I was the last person she thought would return to South Carolina. I agreed with her because when I left, I said I would never move back. Yet, I did move back, and I was very happy that I did.

On November 1, Mom was doing well. She ate a good breakfast and was watching BET. I went to St. Beulah Church today. It was communion Sunday. Rev. Washington's text was titled "The Lord's Supper—What is it?" and was taken from Isaiah 53:5. Service was very good. Mom was doing well when I returned from church. I cooked a good meal, and we ate together. She asked about church, and I reviewed the entire service with her. I even read the scripture that Pastor Washington read. She loved having the word read to her. Her favorite scripture was Psalm 27. That was my favorite also.

November 20, 2009

Stacy would be retiring early and relocating to South Carolina the end of January 2010 to assist in our mother's care. I believed that God sent her to help and just in time. She found a house in the area a few months ago and was able to close on the house today. Since she was unable to get here for the closing, I stood in for her. Stacy was very smart to sell her house in Connecticut before she purchased one in South Carolina. She closed in Connecticut yesterday and both closings went well. I was happy she would be living close by again. I wanted her to know that I understood how much she was sacrificing to come home in January 2010.

November 23, 2009

I took Mom for her follow-up medical appointment with Dr. Shaw. As usual, he reviewed the log of Mom's blood pressure and blood sugar. Mom weighed 178 pounds. Her blood pressure was 185/78, her sugar was 121, and her heart rate was eighty-seven. He made some changes to her medication: Hydrochlorothiazide was increased from 12.5 mg a day to 25 mg a day. The Cardidopa was increased to three times a day. He added Carvedilol (one tablet two times a day) and Furosemide for her congestive heart failure. He discontinued Hydralazine and Benicar.

November 24, 2009

Stacy, her friend Carnel and Stacy's daughter Nicole came home for Thanksgiving and spent some time working on her house. Since she was so busy, I cooked Thanksgiving dinner and invited them over. Stacy, Carnel, Nicole, and Samuel came for dinner. Mom was able to come to the dinner table for our Thanksgiving meal. I cooked a lot of food, and everyone said it was very good. Stacy and Nicole returned to Connecticut on the weekend. Carnel stayed to work on Stacy's house. Today was Gloria's birthday. Happy birthday, Gloria.

December 1, 2009–December 31, 2009

This was a good month for Mom. Her blood pressure was down almost the entire month. It was up a couple of days this month but nothing like in the past. Mom felt good, her appetite was good, and she was full of energy. The home health aide would take Mom for short walks, and she enjoyed being outside. She seemed to be excited about the upcoming holiday season. Just the thought of the approaching holidays gave her something to look forward to. I was happy that she was doing well because George and I were scheduled to go on a cruise this month, and I did not want to leave her feeling unwell. Tracy had promised to stay with Mom while we were on the cruise but that never materialized. Samuel agreed to have Mom stay with him while we were away.

December 4, 2009

Today was George's birthday. Mom was scheduled to go to Samuel's house, but there was a change in plans. Samuel decided to stay at our house with Mom, as it would be more convenient for him and Mom. I thought it was a good idea. Samuel arrived around 11:00 P.M., as we had planned to leave for the cruise very early.

December 5, 2009

It was the day of the cruise. I didn't sleep at all the night before the cruise because of excitement, anxiousness, and just being overly tired. I was up at 1:00 A.M., took a shower, and got dressed; we were scheduled to leave at 2:30 A.M. for the airport in Charlotte, North Carolina, which was a three-hour drive.

We threw our bags in the car, said a little prayer, and off we went at 2:30 A.M. exactly. I didn't like driving in the dark, but I had no choice. It was either me driving or us staying at home. George's eyesight was getting worse by the day. In fact, I truly believed he iwas legally blind. Nevertheless, we were on our way. Our flight was scheduled to leave at 8:05 A.M. I parked the car, and we took the shuttle to the gate. We checked our bags, got our boarding passes, and went through the security checkpoint. We now had to take our shoes off. George had a pacemaker and could not go through the security screening point. Therefore, he had to be searched. George's legs were weak, so we took a ride on a golf cart to the gate. They started loading the plane at 7:40 A.M. We got on and found our seats. I sat next to the window. There was a slight delay because the plane was overweight, but we soon left. It was a good flight, and we didn't have too much turbulence. We landed in Miami about 10:30 A.M. We got our bags and waited for the cruise shuttle bus. Soon we were at the dock with thousands of other people for the cruise. There were two other ships in port, all scheduled to leave at the same time. We met a family on the plane that was scheduled to cruise the next day. It took quite a bit of time, but eventually we were on the ship. The staff had prepared lunch for us, and I was starving. After we ate, we went to our room. It was a larger room than I thought we would have. We had a king-sized bed and lots of storage. We also had a large couch that folded out into another bed. We had an ocean-view cabin with a large window, TV, and bath.

George and I sat on the deck until the ship left port. I took some pictures and waved good-bye to people on the dock. Everyone was waving, so we waved, too. Once the ship took off, we had to do a mandatory lifeboat drill. This took about forty minutes. I knew these drills were important, but I sure hated them. The best thing to do was grin and bear it.

December 7, 2009

Mom had two medical appointments today. Since I was on a cruise, Samuel took her to see Dr Shaw at 9:45 A.M. Samuel said that the nurse asked him, "Where is your book?" as I always had my book with me when I brought Mom in for her appointments. Nevertheless, he took good notes. The nurse also gave him a printout of her exam. Mom weighed 180 pounds. Her blood pressure was 177/71, and her pulse was seventy. Dr. Shaw said that Mom's heart was still enlarged, but it had shrunk some. He didn't know what was causing the cough. He took blood and X-rays. He wanted to do a CAT scan of Mom's chest at some point, but he wanted to see what the pathologist had to say first. He prescribed some antibiotics to try to knock out the fluids in her chest.

Samuel also took Mom to the Hartsville ENT at 1:00 P.M. The doctor cleaned Mom's ears and found some moisture and some wax. She was going to prescribe antibiotics but felt that those prescribed by Dr. Shaw would be enough. If they hadn't cleared up the dampness, they would have had to put in some tubes. Mom also wanted her hearing aids turned up. She said they squelched when she turned them up. The doctor said that turning the aids up inside did the same thing as turning them up outside. It had nothing to do with the squelch. She cleaned the aids and turned them up. She also plugged up the holes in the hearing aids that caused squelching.

December 8, 2009

Dr. Shaw's office called the house and said Mom's blood work showed she was low in vitamin D. He called in a prescription at Walgreens. Samuel picked up the medication.

December 12, 2009

We returned from our cruise today. We got off the ship in Miami around 10:00 A.M. and took the shuttle to the airport. We flew back to Charlotte, and I drove back to Florence. It took over three and one-half hours. It was raining, and the traffic was bad. We got into Florence around 9:00 P.M. Mom was asleep when we got home. Samuel brought me up-to-date on everything. He kept good notes.

December 13, 2009

When Mom came into the kitchen this morning, I was standing at the stove fixing her breakfast. Mom was so happy to see us. She said she had missed us so much. She said Samuel took good care of her. She also said Carnel cooked her some good food. I was pleased with the way Mom looked. It was clear that she was well cared for while I was away.

December 22, 2009

It was a busy day in the Fuller household. George was scheduled to see the neurologist at 10:15 A.M. I also had an appointment with my foot doctor. Therefore, George took himself to his appointment. When he got home, he said he would never go back to see the neurologist again. When I asked why, he said it was a waste of time because the doctor never touched him. He said the doctor walked into the room and said that all his test results were normal. I could not believe that George was never checked. This was a follow-up appointment from George's last hospitalization. I definitely needed to go to all of George's medical appointments.

December 23, 2009

For the first time this month, Mom's blood pressure was up. I checked her blood three times during the day. It ran from 201/84 up to 231/87. I made her rest all morning. When she got up, she wanted to talk to some people in Chesterfield. I dialed the telephone numbers for her, and she spoke with her stepmother and two sisters-in-law. She also called one of her friends, Ms. Burk. You would never know by the way Mom laughed and talked to her family and friend that her pressure was up. Mom bragged so much about how happy she was and talked about what we did for her. Mom was so happy to get news from Chesterfield. When she got off the phone, she said, "Now I can rest because I talked to who I wanted to talk to."

December 25, 2009

Latisha, Calvin, and the children were here for Christmas. Mom spent the Christmas holidays with Stacy. Tracy, Gloria, and Nicole were here for the holidays.

Since Stacy lives around the corner from me, we were all traveling from house to house. We had a good time.

December 28, 2009

Latisha and her family left and returned to Connecticut early this morning. Mom came home today. She said she was glad to be home. She seemed a little upset about something, but I didn't pressure her to talk about it at that time. I checked her blood pressure and blood sugar, and they were both normal. She sat at the table while I cooked, and we ate together. I asked her, "Mom, did you enjoy Christmas?" She said, "Dollie, I'm going to tell you the truth. I didn't enjoy myself at all." I said, "What?" She said, "I sat in my room at night and cried because Gloria was there the entire week, and she did not come in my room once to spend time with me. Tracy was also here, but she never took time to sit and talk with me at all. That hurt me so bad that I cried about it."

Mom appeared to be really hurt, as she was almost in tears. I told Mom that she should have said something to them about how she was feeling. Mom said, "Stacy did everything she could to make me feel at home, but she was so busy unpacking her things, and I didn't want to get in her way." I told Mom that Stacy wanted her there and would have done anything to make her comfortable. Mom said, "She did, and I was comfortable." I called Stacy and told her what Mom said. I later had a chance to talk with Gloria and Tracy and told them what Mom said. When I think about it, we were all in and out of Stacy's house. I spoke with Mom several times during that week, but she never said anything about how she was feeling. I talked to Mom a long time after we ate. I told her that we all loved her and would never do anything to hurt her. I reminded her that she needed to let us know how she was feeling because her feelings were important to all of us.

December 29, 2009

Mom said she felt better this morning. I was happy to hear it because she was very sad last night. Even though her blood pressure was up to 228/95, she ate a good breakfast and said she felt good. Mom seemed okay, but her eyes looked weak. I made her rest most of the day because she had an appointment in Hartsville tomorrow.

December 30, 2009

I checked Mom's pressure this morning before taking her to her ENT appointment. It was 234/96. Mom said she felt good and was in no pain. Stacy and I took Mom to her ENT appointment in Hartsville. The doctor checked Mom's hearing aids and tried to adjust them so Mom could hear better. Mom had been saying that the hearing aids were set too low, and she was having a difficult time hearing. The doctor took time to reset the aids and kept asking Mom if they were all right. Mom said, "Oh yes, I can hear good now." Stacy and I kept asking "Mom, are you sure they are all right?" Mom told us that the hearing aids were much better, and she could hear really well. But as soon as we left the room and were in the elevator, Mom started complaining. She said that the doctor turned her hearing aids down too low. Stacy snapped, so much so that you could see her blood vessels. She said enunciating every syllable, "Mom, the doctor kept asking you if they were okay, and you said yes. We can't tell the doctor if they are too low or too high because the hearing aids are in your ears, not ours." I was hurting from trying not to laugh. We were right there, and we all asked Mom if they were okay. Mom said she could hear much better while in the room. Now she said they were too low. This did not surprise me because I was used to Mom going back and forth, and I thought Stacy was too. However, neither of us expected this today—we were actually shocked. My entire insides were hysterical with laughter, but I was not about to let Stacy know how funny she was because she was pretty upset.

We also took Mom to Safe at Home Medical Equipment and Supplies to get her diabetic shoes. The shoes did not fit because of Mom's high instep. We had to send the shoes back. We ordered another pair of shoes.

December 31, 2009

Mom's blood pressure was 201/100 this morning. I increased her medication as instructed and had her rest for a couple of hours. I rechecked it later, and it was back to normal.

Chapter 9

***

It's a New Year

"Confess your faults one to another, and pray one for another, that ye may be healed. The effectual fervent prayer of a righteous man availeth much."
—James 5:16

The New Year started off with Mom's blood pressure going up and down again. It was running 127/64 to 207/78. Her sugar was also out of control and went as high as 279. I continued to check her blood every day and kept the doctor abreast of her condition. I made sure Mom took all her medicine and on time. I cooked for her daily and made sure she had a balanced meal every day. In addition to Mom's unstable medical condition, George's health was also declining. Stacy returned to Connecticut to complete her two weeks' notice.

George kept falling and his driving was becoming more and more unsafe. His sight in one eye was totally gone and he was probably legally blind in the other eye. I started talking to my siblings about an alternative plan for Mom. One of them may have to take her (assisted living program vs a nursing home). Even discussing these alternatives was difficult for us, as we never wanted Mom to go into a nursing home. What would that do to our mother and what would it do to us if we had to make that decision? At first I thought, *"Maybe Tracy or Stacy could take Mom, but their health was poor, and they might not be able to care for Mom either."*

I told my siblings that it was becoming almost impossible for me to take care of Mom and George. When George needed me, I felt I was neglecting Mom, and when she needed me, I was neglecting George. There were times when I was up all night with Mom or with George. My health was feeling the strain of juggling everything for which I was responsible, and I had never felt so tired. Additionally, my doctor told me I was neglecting myself. If I maintained my current routine, I wouldn't be here to take care of anyone. I talked to Tracy in the past about taking care of Mom if anything happened to me. At first she said she would do her best. However, later she said that her health was so bad that she would not be able to care for Mom. As long as I could manage Mom and George, I would continue to take care of them, but I didn't know how long my health would allow me to do this. We needed to explore an alternative plan while Mom was doing well.

Dollie's Diary

***

January 8, 2010

I took Mom to see Dr. Shaw today. Mom weighed 176.5 pounds. Her blood pressure was better today (141/71). The doctor was still concerned about her unstable blood pressure and sugar. There were no changes made to her medication today. He asked me to continue to check her sugar and pressure daily. Mom had a good day today, but I have learned to take one day at a time.

January 10, 2010

I took George for his eye appointment this morning. According to the doctor, his eyes have not improved, and he still had a lot of pressure behind his eyes. His sight was so poor that he could barely see. I was worried about his sight and the fact that he was still driving. He refused to give it up. Taking care of him right now was sometimes more difficult than taking care of Mom, and she could see that it was affecting my health. Mom repeatedly told me, "Dollie, George is sick. He is worse than me. You can't take care of both of us. You need to put me in a nursing home." I never wanted to put Mom in a nursing home, but if it ever got to a point where I could no longer take care of them both, what other options would I have? I had no alternative plan. I talked to Samuel about it, and he said, "I'll be honest with you—you lasted longer that I thought you would. We do need to start talking about what will happen to Mom if you can no longer take care of her. If George's health continues to go in the direction that it is going, it will be sooner than you think. Whether it happens now or two years from now, we need to start exploring our options."

January 11, 2010

I took Mom to get her toenails cut. She complained all the way to the appointments. She said, "Dollie, this is too far to go. Why can't you find me a doctor in Florence?" Mom was extremely irritable all the way to Cheraw and back, but I had no choice. She said her toes hurt and needed to be seen. I spent hours on the telephone trying to find a podiatrist in Florence or the surrounding areas, but they would not accept Mom's insurance. I told her that I would try again.

George also had an eye appointment today. Since I took Mom to Cheraw, he had to take himself. This was bad because I needed to go with him to all his medical appointments. When Mom and I got home, I was a little worried because George should have been home by then. I tried to reach him on his cell phone, but he had left the phone at home. Mom kept asking "Where's George?" His appointment was early in the day, but it was late afternoon when he finally got home. I asked him, "Where did you go?" He said he got lost and ended up somewhere in Society Hill or Darlington. At one time, he had no idea where he was. He said he finally recognized where he was and found his way back home. This was beginning to be even more of a concern. I would need to take him wherever he needed to go.

January 13, 2010–January 16, 2010

George and I decided to go to Connecticut with Carnel to get Stacy. She completed her notice and was now retired. She will be relocating to South Carolina. I helped Carnel drive his van to Connecticut and would help Stacy drive her car back. This was a good break from everything. Samuel stayed with Mom.

January 17, 2010–January 21, 2010

Stacy was now living in Florence. She purchased a three-bedroom, three-bath house around the corner from George, Mom, and me. The house was beautiful with an enclosed backyard and lots of privacy. Stacy was staying close to home, as she had to unpack everything and get the house the way she wanted it. She was also trying to find her way around Florence. One day I went with Stacy and Carnel to City Hall and the Department of Motor

Vehicles to show them where they were. She said she liked Florence and was happy about her retirement. I want her to know that I understand how much she sacrificed in order to come home and help with Mom at this time.

January 22, 2010

I called cardiology associates to complete George's telephone pacemaker check. I tried to show him how to do it himself, but he was unable to grasp the procedure. I did the check, and it went well. No concerns were noted.

Sunday, January 24, 2010

We were all still searching for a church home. George, Stacy, Carnel, and I visited First Christian Church in Florence this morning. The pastor took his text from 1 Samuel 3:1–10 and 19–21. His text was "Is God calling you and are you listening for his voice?" The home health aide stays with Mom for three hours on Sundays. This allows us more freedom to go to church and really enjoy the services. Even though Mom's pressure was up and down all month, she felt good all week.

January 25, 2010

I took George to see his primary physician today. He prescribed Aricept (5 mg/day) for agitation, memory loss, and to help his thinking ability. He said George's iron saturation was down and prescribed Tandem capsules three times a week to help prevent iron deficiency. He also prescribed some vitamin D3. He would schedule George for a colonoscopy.

<u>Sunday, January 31, 2010</u>

Mom continued to say she felt good all week. Each day she talked about going to church on Sunday. This morning she got up early, ate breakfast, and said, "I'm going to church today." I called the home health aide and told her not to come. Mom not only wanted to go to church, she wanted to go to my brother Samuel's church. I called Stacy and Carnel, and they said they would go. We all got ready and went to Centerville Missionary Baptist Church. Samuel was surprised. The male chorus sang, and Mom enjoyed seeing Samuel in the choir. We all enjoyed the services very much. The pastor took his text "Little Faith" from St. Matthew 14:22–33. We all loved hearing him preach.

<u>February 1, 2010–February 28, 2010</u>

This month was no different with Mom's blood pressure. It was going up and down again, running as high as 218/113. I checked her blood pressure daily and kept the doctor up-to-date. Mom kept saying she felt good and was in no pain at all. Yet, I could see her dragging a little. In fact, she would say she didn't feel like coming to the table and was eating more meals in her room. Mom talked about her time getting close more frequently now. I tried to spend as much time with her as possible. I told her more and more how much I loved her. She didn't look sick to me, but she might have known something that we didn't know. We all heard what she was saying and wanted to do whatever we could to make her happy. Stacy stopped by the house to see Mom daily. Mom enjoyed having Stacy spend time with her. Stacy took on the responsibility of taking care of Mom's hair. She would comb and braid Mom hair two to three times a week. We told Mom that she looked cute. Mom loved having her hair combed.

February 4, 2010

Today was Mom's birthday. I gave her a new white hat and a cream two-piece dress. She was so happy to get the new outfit. She said she would wear it when she goes back to Grove Baptist Church. Mom wanted to look her best at all times. She was a proud woman and took pains with her appearance.

February 11, 2010

George had a medical appointment with his primary physician this morning. I was unable to go to the doctor with him today, as I had to stay with Mom, so I sent a note informing the doctor of George's symptoms and complaints because I knew he would forget. I told the doctor that he complained that his foot got cold at night and that he lost his balance at times, which meant he might have something going on with his inner ear. I also noted that his memory loss was getting worse, he became extremely explosive at times, and he had difficulty sleeping at night. I also sent my phone number in case the doctor needed additional information. When George returned from the doctor, I asked if he gave the doctor my note. He said, "Yes. The doctor wants to make sure you come to my next appointment." I said okay. I took the appointment card and put the date and time in my book.

Sunday, February 14, 2010

We were still visiting different churches. George, Carnel, Stacy, and I went to Monumental Missionary Baptist Church in Florence this morning. The morning message was "The Lost Sheep of Israel" taken from St. Matthew 10:1–7. The home health aide came today. She was at the home for three hours. Mom said she felt good today.

February 16, 2010

I called Hartville ENT this morning about Mom's hearing aid volume control knob needing repair. Mom turned the knob so hard that she broke it off. We looked everywhere for the knob but could not find it. I was told to drop the hearing aid off this afternoon. I drove to Hartville ENT and dropped the hearing aid off at the front desk.

February 18, 2010

George's doctor ordered test at Carolina Hospital. He had to be there at 7:30 A.M. for registration, 8:00 A.M. for a CAT scan, and 8:30 A.M. for a carotid study. At 9:30 A.M., they put a heart monitor on him for one day. He had to wear the heart monitor all night and return the next morning to have it removed.

February 19, 2010

George returned to Carolina Hospital to have the heart monitor removed.

Sunday, February 21, 2010

George, Carnel, Stacy, and I visited Trinity Baptist Church this morning. The members were very friendly. The pastor took his text from St. Luke 4:1–13. His text was "Conflict in the Wilderness." Even though we enjoyed the services, this was not the church for us.

February 24, 2010

Stacy and I took Mom to Hartville ENT today at 10:00 A.M. The appointment went well. Mom got her hearing aid back, but the knob was still off.

February 25, 2010

I took George to see his primary physician today. He wanted to make sure that I also came to this appointment because he wanted me to know what was going on with George. The test results showed that George's health was a little worse right now. I had noticed that his balance was really off, and his sight seemed to be getting worse. George was totally in denial, as he felt that everything was all right. Mom was worried about him. She would jump when he stumbled or reach out to move something out of his way when she saw him coming. George would get so upset. When he stumbled, and Mom jumped, he would say, "I'm not going to fall. You need to stop doing that." One night he told me, "You need to tell your mother to stop moving things for me. I can see them." I told Mom to look the other way when she saw him coming, but it was her nature to reach out and try to help. There were times when I felt I was right in the middle and didn't know how to handle it. I agreed with Mom, and I would jump, too. Even though George felt he was okay, Mom and I had our doubts. The doctor told George that he could send him to therapy, but George refused. The doctor then said, "If you don't go to therapy, then you need to walk around the block at least twice a day." George said he'd rather walk.

March 1, 2010–March 31, 2010

Mom's blood pressure was still up and down. However, on the days when it was high, it would go down by the afternoon and stay down for two or three days at a time. Her sugar seemed to be staying down better than before. Mom did not seem to have very much energy this month. I was beginning to worry because the spells were more frequent and she appeared somewhat weaker than normal. She still came to the table when she felt like it, but when she felt too weak, I would take her food to her room. When Mom first moved in with me, cooking for her was easy because she loved everything I cooked. I spent time learning what she enjoyed and tried to cook it often. Today Stacy came over and brought Mom some fish, potatoes, and fritters. Mom loved that and ate it all. This was a big help because I did not have to think about what she was going to eat today. Stacy was always thinking of ways to help me with Mom and I loved having her so close.

March 10, 2010

We received word that my cousin had passed away. He was living in New York, but they planned to bury him at Grove Baptist Church. His funeral was scheduled for Friday, March 19, 2010 at 2:30 P.M. Mom wanted all of us to go. Mom was always concerned about the family and wanted us to be supportive of each other. We tried to offer support as much as we could.

March 16, 2010

I took Mom for her medical appointment with Dr. Shaw. Mom weighed 177.2 pounds. Her blood pressure was 132/72 and her pulse was sixty-two. I talked to the doctor about Mom having more frequent spells and told him that her cough had gotten worse. They did blood work and X-rays for the cough. Dr. Shaw wanted to send Mom to McLeod Hospital for an ultrasound of her throat and an MRI. Dr. Shaw would schedule the appointment and get back to us with the date and time. He also changed Mom's Parkinson medication to three times a day at separate times.

March 18, 2010

I received a call from Dr. Shaw's nurse regarding the results of the blood work. Dr. Shaw prescribed Pravastatin for high cholesterol. He would call it in to Walgreens.

March 19, 2010

My cousin was buried today at Grove Baptist Church. Mom wasn't feeling well, so I stayed home with her. Samuel attended the funeral alone.

Sunday, March 21, 2010

George and I went to St. Beulah Baptist Church this morning for regular worship service. The service was a little longer than usual, as they were celebrating the church's eighty-sixth anniversary and had a guest pastor and his congregation delivering the services. Stacy's daughter Nicole was visiting her mother from Connecticut and stayed with Mom while we were at church.

After church, we had dinner at Stacy's house. Tracy was also visiting from North Carolina. Mom said she felt weak and did not feel like coming out, so we told her we would bring her a plate. Carnel played a trick on Mom. He fixed her a tiny little baby plate and sent it over. Nicole and I laughed when Mom saw the size of the plate. It was a tiny little saucer with only about four teaspoons of food on it. Mom looked at the plate in amazement—she didn't know what to say. We laughed so hard that we cried. When we gave Mom the real plate, she said, "Wait till I see him." Mom was happy to get the second plate. It was so funny. Mom enjoyed that food. She said, "That man knows he can cook."

Samuel was scheduled to be ordained as deacon at Centerville Baptist Church at 4:00 P.M. today. We all planned to attend. The home health aide was scheduled to come and stay with Mom. I kept waiting for the home health aide, but she never showed. I called her on her cell phone to remind her but never got through. I told everyone that they should go on, as it was getting late, and I would stay with Mom. Stacy offered to stay, but I felt she should go because her daughter was visiting, and it would be nice if she went to the ordination with her. I know she did not mind staying with Mom but neither did I. When I took on the responsibility of taking care of Mom, I accepted the fact that I might have to change my plans to stay at home with her or George for that matter. This was part of my life now, and I didn't mind.

Before leaving for the church, Tracy got a phone call from her friends stating they had to pick her up early, so she was also unable to go to the ordination service. So we both stayed home with Mom until Tracy's ride came to pick her up. Her friends came around 6:00 P.M., and Tracy returned to North Carolina.

March 24, 2010

The closing on 6649 Stagecoach Road in Effingham, South Carolina, was today. When we purchased this house, we thought it was the perfect house for us. However, after Mom came to live with us, we knew that the house would not work for her. Therefore, we put it on the market and purchased another house to have more space for Mom. We have been juggling both houses for a year. I thank God the house was finally sold.

March 25, 2010

Mom wasn't feeling too good today. Her blood pressure was up to 224/94, her pulse was sixty-nine, and her blood sugar was 129. She was scheduled to go to McLeod Hospital for an MRI and ultrasound. Stacy and I took her for the tests. We took her wheelchair, as Mom was very weak, and the hospital was too large for her to try to walk. Mom's home health aide also went with us but left when her time was up. After the tests, we took Mom to get something to eat.

After I got home, I received a call from Dr. Shaw. He said the MRI showed that Mom had a stroke about a week earlier. I couldn't believe he had gotten the result of the test that quickly and was calling us already. He wanted to start Mom on a new medication (Plavix) and an aspirin a day. This would reduce the risk of her having another stroke.

March 26, 2010

Lately I had been having problems with my eyes. At times, I couldn't see at all. One night I woke up to go to the bathroom, and my sight was totally gone for a few minutes. I kept shutting and opening my eyes in an effort to regain my vision. It frightened me at first because the same thing had happened to Mom. Maybe it was a way for me to feel what Mom was feeling when she went blind. I scheduled an eye exam at Carolina Center for Sight and was told that my eyes had gotten worse in the last year. The doctor further stated that I might need cataract surgery next year. I thought, *"I refuse to accept that diagnosis."* He wanted me to try some new glasses and see how they would do in the meantime. He gave me a prescription for new glasses. I asked the Lord for healing because I know that by his stripes we are healed.

"Is any sick among you? Let him call for the elders of the church; and let them pray over him, anointing him with oil in the name of the Lord." —James 5:14 (KJV)

March 29, 2010

I took Mom for her follow-up appointment with Dr. Shaw this morning. She weighed 176.8. Her blood pressure was 152/71, and her pulse was fifty-six. Dr. Shaw took an X-ray of Mom's chest because of her cough. The X-rays showed that Mom had bronchitis and a touch of pneumonia. He put Mom on more antibiotics (Avelox, 400 mg/Day). I thought, *"How much more can Mom endure?"* I called Stacy and brought her up-to-date.

April 1, 2010–April 30, 2010

Mom struggled this month, as she did not feel well at all. She tried to come to the table for breakfast, but she was just too weak. She kept apologizing, but I told her that it was all right. I had no problem taking her food to her room. It was clear that she was sick. I felt bad for her. If I had the power, I would make her feel better. It was clear that her health was deteriorating. I tried cooking her favorite foods, but on certain days, she ate very little. Her blood pressure was up and down all month. It went from 142/71 to 224/94. Mom appeared to be getting weaker and weaker. We knew she was sick because she looked it and did not have enough energy to do anything. Stacy had been coming daily to take Mom for walks, but Mom started refusing to go. In fact, she stopped going in and out of the house because she was just that weak. We were very worried about Mom's condition.

The home health aide gave me some Pediasure, and Mom seemed to love the drink. I started worrying when her appetite changed, as she refused breakfast at times and would only drink a Pediasure or eat a piece of fruit. I started asking her what she wanted to eat because she would refuse everything. She said certain foods bothered her stomach and she did not want to throw up. Mom even refused her favorite foods at times, and I became desperate. If she said she wanted anything I did not have in the house, I would run to the store to get it but that didn't happen often. I talked with Stacy and Samuel about her health. They were also worried. Stacy would cook certain things and bring them over, but at times, we were both baffled. We didn't know what to do.

April 6, 2010 – April 9, 2010

Today Mom had an appointment to have her toenails cut. Mom got up early and ate some breakfast, and the home health aide helped her get dressed. Stacy picked us up, as she was driving us to the appointment in Cheraw. Mom got sick and became nauseated on the ride. Stacy had to stop three times because Mom kept throwing up. Mom got so sick that we had to turn around and take her back home. We got her some ginger ale, but that did not help at all. After she got home, she rested the remainder of the day. I rescheduled her appointment. Stacy and I were so worried that we stayed close the rest of the week. Mom looked sick and was eating very little. Stacy and I tried cooking her favorite foods, but she said it bothered her stomach. Mom was scheduled to see Dr. Shaw on Monday, April 12, 2010.

April 10, 2010

Mom got up early this morning and said she felt good today. After breakfast she was able to sit outside for a little while. She ate all her food and asked for more. She actually came to the table. Stacy and I were so happy she felt better. Mom also looked much better and she had a little more energy. This was a big improvement and we were very pleased.

Today was my birthday. I was now sixty-five years old. I received flowers from my daughter and her family. They were beautiful. Mom kept looking at the flowers and kept saying how much she loved them, so I gave them to her so she could enjoy their beauty. I placed them on her dresser. She was so pleased. I didn't think my daughter would mind my giving them to her. Latisha, Stacy, and Samuel never forgot my birthday. I got a beautiful picture frame from Stacy. It was a double frame so I put both Mom's and Dad's pictures in it. When I looked at the frame, I always thought of Stacy, Mom, and Dad. Samuel invited me to dinner and since Mom was feeling better today, I accepted. He took me and his girlfriend Marie to one of his favorite restaurants. Marie and I shared the same birth date. We had a good meal and enjoyed each other's company. Stacy stayed with Mom while I was out.

April 11, 2010

George and I joined St. Beulah Baptist Church today, a day after my sixty-fifth birthday. I felt so relieved because I belonged somewhere again. I always hated walking up to join a church. I was happy it was over.

April 12, 2010

Stacy and I took Mom to see Dr. Shaw for a follow-up appointment this morning. Mom weighed 177.6. Her blood pressure was 151/71, and her pulse was sixty-three. Dr. Shaw expressed concern about Mom's blood pressure. He told Mom absolutely no church, no crowds, and no company. We told him that at times, Mom's speech was somewhat garbled, and we could hardly understand what she was saying. He said that she was still a very sick woman. He said Mom's immune system was weak, and she couldn't fight anything off. She needed to stay put, as he couldn't seem to keep up with it. It kept coming back. Mom still had bronchitis and pneumonia. He gave me prescriptions for refills on Avelox (400 mg), Furosemide (40 mg) and Glipizide (5 mg).

Sunday, April 18, 2010

We went to church today. I enjoyed the services. Rev. Washington preached from St. Luke 10:17–20. His text was "You got a license to praise the Lord." The home health aide stayed with Mom.

Chapter 10

***

George has a Stroke

"But they that wait upon the LORD shall renew their strength; they shall mount up with wings as eagles; they shall run, and not be weary; and they shall walk, and not faint." —Isaiah 40:31

April 19, 2010

George woke up this morning with slurred speech. His balance was also a little more unsteady than normal. I knew immediately that he had had a stroke during the night. I told him to get dressed because I was taking him to the hospital. I called the doctor first regarding his symptoms and was told to take him straight to the hospital. As expected, he did not want to go, but I insisted. He thought he was all right. When I reached the hospital, I checked him in, and the doctor immediately checked him. His speech was so bad that the doctor could not understand anything he was saying. To be honest, I couldn't either. I answered all the questions. The doctor sent him for a

CAT scan, chest X-ray, and blood work. After the test, he returned to say that George had to be admitted, as his blood pressure was still elevated.

My first thought was, *"What about Mom?"* The home health aide was scheduled to leave soon. I called my sister, Stacy and asked if she would pick Mom up at home and take her to her house. She agreed. She later called back and stated that Mom's speech was somewhat distorted, and she was very weak. She mentioned that Carnel said that if it were his mom, he would not move her, but she could do what she wanted. Stacy decided to let Mom stay at the house but stayed there with her until I got home. When I got home from the hospital, Stacy had fed Mom, and she was set for the night. I took a shower and went to bed.

April 20, 2010

Day two. George remains hospitalized. I got up early this morning, made Mom's breakfast before the home health aide came and checked in with Mom. Mom seemed to be doing okay today. Today was the home health aide's long day. She would be at the house for five hours. This would be a big help to me. I gave the home health aide some instructions when she arrived and was off to the hospital by 8:15 A.M.

When I arrived at the hospital, George was very agitated. He wanted to go home. George was admitted yesterday after having a stroke. The doctor wanted to monitor him for a few days and run some tests. His speech was slurred, and his balance was off when he woke up that morning. George was scheduled for two tests (echocardiogram and ultrasound of his neck) today. They came and took him down late that morning for the test. When he returned, he asked, "What are we waiting on?" I told him, "We are waiting for you to be discharged." You can't just walk out of the hospital without being discharged. I guess you can, but you shouldn't. He had not even seen the doctor and wanted to leave. He was visibly upset. He was so mad that he threw the bed blanket across the room. I merely sat there and watched him act out. I said nothing. In fact, I acted as though I saw or heard nothing. I was not going to allow his behavior to stress me out any more than I already was.

I stayed at the hospital all day. Stacy stayed with Mom after the home health aide left. I was just sitting at the hospital waiting for answers. It gave me time to think about my situation. I finally realized something that hurt so deeply. I couldn't take care of two sick people effectively. George and Mom were both sick. I was just one person. I felt that I was spread too thin these days. I had help but not the kind I needed. Stacy and Samuel were both available, and they both helped a lot, but I still felt stressed. I appreciate what they do to help me out, but they get to go home at night. There were times when I had to get up three and four times during the night for Mom or George.

I felt so overwhelmed. Was it me? Was I being selfish? No, it wasn't me. I was human and felt worn out. I was tired.

By the time I got home that night from the hospital, I was in tears. I went straight to the bathroom to wash my face, so Stacy and Mom couldn't tell how upset I was. Trying to take care of George at the hospital and Mom at night was getting to me. I kept breaking down. I cried almost all night long. I was exhausted. I started getting sick because I hurt when I urinated. I was stressed to the max.

I called Samuel to ask if Mom could stay with him a couple of days, but he was not at home. I left a message for him to call me when he got home. Stacy left to go home, so I decided to go out and get the mail. When I walked out of the house, Stacy was taking the mail out of my mailbox for me. I thought, *"I don't want her to see my eyes—then she will know I've been crying."* She asked me how things were with George. At that moment, I couldn't hold it in. Tears rolled down my face.

I told Stacy how George was acting out at the hospital and how trying to balance everything with Mom and George was difficult for me. My body was reacting to the stress. I told her that I had called Samuel to see if he could keep Mom for a few days, but he wasn't home.

Stacy said, "I'll keep Mom if she wants to come." Stacy was right about Mom not wanting to stay at her house. Stacy tried hard to make Mom feel at home, but Mom just did not want to stay there. Mom made every excuse in the book not to go there. When she did go, she would tell the home health aide that she wanted to go home. She would say negative things about being there and at one time, she hit the chair with her fist in anger. I knew Mom did not want to be there, but I would feel better if I knew she was safe and well cared for. This would allow me to focus on George and not worry about her. Samuel also called and said he would pick Mom up immediately if I wanted him to. They were both willing to do whatever they could to help me, but knowing that did not stop me from feeling overwhelmed. What should I do? I tried to explain my needs to everyone, but I was unable to articulate my feelings. Taking care of two people was beginning to affect my health. We needed to sit down as a family and talk about other options. Where should we go from here? In the meantime, Mom would go to Stacy's house tomorrow and stay until George was released from the hospital.

April 21, 2010

George had been in the hospital for three days now. His blood pressure was still high (171/101). His primary physician wanted him to stay in the hospital until his pressure stabilized. George said he slept better last night. I didn't sleep at all because I had problems with my bladder. I fixed Mom's pills and made her breakfast before I left for the hospital. The home health aide was there for only two hours today. I asked her to take Mom to Stacy's house this morning before she left. I knew Mom would not want to go there, but she could not stay in the house alone. I later called home to check on Mom. The home health aide had already taken her to Stacy's house. This was good. I called Stacy's house to check on Mom. I was told that Mom fell, but she was okay. Samuel and Carnel picked her up.

The nurse came in and checked George's blood pressure. It was very high. I went out of the room and spoke to the nurse. She said the doctor would not send him home with his blood pressure that high, as he could have another stroke. I went back in the room and said, "You ask me what we are waiting for. We are waiting for your blood pressure to go down. You need to calm down and accept the fact that you are in the hospital and not in a grave. Be patient. You are the one controlling your blood pressure, as you keep getting upset about not going home and sending your blood pressure sky high." George immediately calmed down, and said, "If I have to stay, I'll stay." The doctor later came into the room and said that all the test results were normal. They need to get his blood pressure down before he could go home because he might have another stroke if it remained as high as it was. George needed to calm down, suck it up, and stay put until his pressure was back to normal.

While at the hospital I called my doctor to schedule an appointment for tomorrow. She said she could see me at 10:45 A.M. I left the hospital around 5:00 P.M. After checking in with Stacy regarding Mom, I fixed myself something to eat and settled down for the night.

April 22, 2010

I woke up early this morning and was at the hospital around 8:05 A.M. Last night was different for me, as I was at home alone. It was also better than the night before with regard to the urinary tract infection.

George had been hospitalized since April 19. George and the nurse told me that his blood pressure was back to normal. George's speech was also back to normal. The plan was for him to be discharged today. I left the hospital at 10:00 A.M. to see my doctor regarding the bladder problem. She said I had a urinary tract infection and gave me antibiotics. She said that the UTI could be caused by stress. I told her that I had enough stress right now to bring on anything. I returned to the hospital, but George was still not ready for discharge, so I went to get my prescription filled. I returned to his room and waited for the doctor.

I met with George's doctor before his discharge. He said the CAT scan showed a change in his brain's cognitive functioning. It is at the moderate level at this time. He said he should not drive, as his functioning wouldn't allow him to keep himself or others safe. His blood pressure was down to normal, and both CAT scans were normal. He was sending George home to see how he did that week. He wanted to see George in his office next Friday. He said he would discuss the driving in more detail at that time. He gave me a copy of George's CAT scans for me to read.

George was discharged today with *no driving* written on the discharge instructions. The doctor also gave George a prescription that stated no driving. I had never seen that before. George was not a happy camper. It was clear that I had my work cut out for me. I thought about having two sick people who didn't want to listen. Mom was already hardheaded because she felt she could still do the things she had done in the past. She would try to clear the table and wash dishes when she could hardly stand up by herself. Samuel and I would get on her about that, but she would not listen. I often caught her walking with her cane, instead of using her walker. Mom had fallen more than once in the past without warning because her legs would just give out on her. On one hand, I was afraid for her, but then again, I never wanted her to feel helpless. She wanted to maintain her independence, and she often talked about living alone again one day. She would say, "Dollie, let me do for myself as long as I can. One day, I want my own place again." She truly wanted her independence, and I never wanted to take that away from her.

George was worse than Mom. He felt in his heart that he could perform the same as he did when he was thirty years old. His sight was poor and his driving had been bad for years, but you could never convince him of that. I knew they both needed me, and I will continue to try to be there for them.

Chapter 11

***

Mom's Spells

"That if thou shalt confess with thy mouth the Lord Jesus, and shalt believe in thine heart that God hath raised him from the dead, thou shalt be saved." —Romans 10:9

One negative thing about caring for the elderly or any individual who needs in-home services is having different people in your house all the time. Everyone is not honest. You are not privy to worker's background checks when they are sent to the house. You have to rely on the agencies to screen these workers. When Mom lived alone, one of the home health aides checked in early in the morning and left the house until her time was up. She returned in time to sign-out. She did not do anything for my mother. I found out by accident. Mom did not want to say anything because she wanted to stay in her own home, but she finally admitted that the aide was never there. I reported it to my mother's case manager, and the person was fired. The problem was that I should never have to report anyone to get them to do their job. One aide actually laid on Mom's bed and went to sleep. Mom was babysitting her. Another aide stole my mother's jewelry and clothes. We never knew what was taken. One person charged personal things at the store where my mother had an account. We got bills for things that we knew our mother wasn't buying. We confronted this person, but we were never reimbursed. Another aide was extremely cruel to my mother when they were alone, but treated her well when we were around. When I found out, I fired her on the spot. I knew my mother had a mouth on her, and it got to me sometimes, but I would just walk away. This person would get angry and argue with her. Mom said, "I talk to her, and she won't even answer me. I asked for water, and she won't move. She is mean to me." I confronted the worker and told her that we couldn't use her anymore. No one mistreats my mother. I also reported her to the agency. If you can't treat a person with kindness and respect, then you should not be in the social service field.

It took a long time, but the home health aide my mother had this time was someone she cared about very much. She would tell the aide things that she would not tell us. Sometimes I felt that Mom wanted the aide to tell us how she felt, but other times we knew she did not want us to know. There were times when we had to ask the aide how Mom truly felt about something. Mom talked about all of us to the aide, whether it was good or bad. We actually learned that Mom didn't want to stay at Stacy's house from the home health aide. One night during our talks, I asked Mom about it. Mom admitted that she did not want to stay there. When asked why, Mom said, "You don't understand. If I stayed there, it's like I am agreeing with their living arrangements. God is not pleased with the way they are living." Mom seemed a little upset at the time, so I acknowledged what she said and left it at that.

April 25, 2010

For the last three nights, my sleep had been interrupted. I was totally exhausted. George kept me up for two nights. He was having pain in his foot and legs. He seemed to be okay at the moment. Last night was Mom's turn. As soon as I drifted off to sleep, I heard her calling me, "Dollie, come in here." I ran to the room, and she said, "Dollie, I'm sick. Will you turn on the light?" I did. She said, "I believe the Lord is coming for me. I keep going in and out." When I asked her what she meant, she said, "My sight, it keeps going in and out." I grabbed the blood pressure machine and checked her blood. It was a little high. I checked her sugar, and it was normal. I asked if she wanted to go to the hospital, and she said, "Let me just rest a while. I'll be all right." I stayed with her as she rested. After a few minutes, she said her sight was returning, and the spell was leaving her. She told me to go back to bed. When I didn't leave right away, she said, "Dollie, I'm all right. Go back to bed. I want to be alone with the Lord." I left the room but I didn't go back to bed right away. I couldn't sleep at all. I checked on her every hour all night long, and each time I checked, she appeared to be resting all right.

Early that morning, I checked in on Mom. She said that she felt better, but she was still very weak. She said, "Now Dollie, you need to go on to church now—don't think you have to stay here with me." I said, "Okay, Mom." However, I wasn't about to leave her alone today. I called Stacy to see if she was going to church, and she said she wasn't because she wanted to spend some time with Mom this morning. I made Mom's breakfast and got dressed for church. Stacy stayed with Mom.

George and I attended St. Beulah this morning. Rev. Washington preached from St. Luke 18:1. His text was "How persistent is your faith?" The choir sang, "If it had not been for the Lord on my side, tell me where would I be—where would I be?" I really needed to hear that today. I cried through the whole song. The spirit was high this morning. I needed to be in the presence of the Lord. In his sermon, the pastor talked about consistent prayer. He said when you continue to pray and keep on praying, it involves effort. I know I have been praying consistently.

When George and I got home, Stacy had already fed Mom, and she was resting. Stacy said that she enjoyed spending time with Mom. Mom later told me, "I enjoyed Stacy today, but I still think something is wrong with her." I told Mom that Stacy was fine. She said, "I know when my children are sick—you just wait and see." I said, "Okay, Mom." I told Stacy later that Mom still thought she was sick. Stacy said that she was still not feeling well, and she didn't know what was wrong with her—maybe she was just tired from trying to get things done. I told her that I was tired, too. Taking care of Mom and George was beginning to affect my health. I was up all day and all night. My body was not getting the rest that it needed to function. If something happened to me, who would take care of Mom and George? Stacy agreed that we needed an alternative plan.

Mom had in her mind that one day she would like to have a place of her own. We often left Mom in the house alone for an hour or two at a time when she was doing well. We knew she wanted time to herself. She did well on her own. She told Tracy and Stacy that she liked being left in the house alone, as she wanted her privacy and independence. Stacy and I talked about an assisted living program or a supervised apartment for Mom. They are costly but very nice. The positive thing about an assisted living program is that Mom would always have someone there for her. She would have supervision twenty-four hours a day. Stacy and I both agreed that we did not want Mom to ever go to a nursing home. We decided to talk with Gloria, Tracy, and Samuel about these programs because they will all have to assist with the cost.

April 26, 2010

Stacy and I took Mom to see Dr. Shaw for a follow-up medical appointment. I told him about Mom's spells becoming more frequent. She had a spell last night where her sight was going in and out. She thought she was dying. I took her blood pressure and it was elevated. Mom weighed was 177.6. Her blood pressure was 143/71, and her heart rate was sixty-five. Mom said she reached up to turn the light on and got dizzy. Dr. Shaw said it was because of her circulation (pleural effusion). He told her not to reach up anymore. She had an X-ray, blood work, and urine test. He reviewed her medication and made some adjustments. He said the chest X-ray showed about two inches of fluid on the side of her chest. He prescribed Paxil to calm her nerves. I filled the prescriptions at Walgreens.

April 27, 2010

Mom was doing well this morning. Her blood pressure was normal. She ate a good breakfast and planned to take a little walk with the home health aide. Stacy and I went shopping. Mom never let up about eventually having her own place. She said she would love to be around people her own age. If Mom's health is okay, we would support having her in a healthy and supportive environment with people her own age. While driving, Stacy and I talked about an assisted living program. We wanted to compare an assisted living program with a nursing home, so we stopped by both. The assisted living program was beautiful and well maintained. Mom would love living there. The nursing home was depressing, and we did not like it at all. We knew right away that it was out of the question. If Mom was going anywhere, it was in an assisted living program. We discussed it with Samuel, Tracy, and Gloria. They agreed to assist with the cost. When we got home, we told Mom about it. She was so excited that she wanted to go right away to see the place. The assisted living programs are very nice but costly. We took her to the program, and she loved it. Now that she likes it, how do we pay for it?

April 28, 2010

Mom felt good this morning. After breakfast, Mom asked to go to Stacy's house today. I told her that I would walk her over as soon as I got dressed. I called Stacy to alert her of Mom's wishes. Stacy said it was fine, as she was just working in the yard. Mom was still talking about the assisted living program. She told me, "Once I make friends, you and Stacy don't have to come see me every day." Mom seemed very happy about getting her own place and going to Stacy's house today. She even told Stacy that she might stay all night. However, as the day progressed, she started making excuses and said, "I guess I have to go home because Dollie didn't bring my nightgown." Stacy already had one of her gowns, so her excuse was invalid. She did stay at Stacy's house that night.

April 29, 2010

Mom had another spell early this morning at Stacy's house. She told the home health aide that she was sick all night but did not want to wake Stacy. Mom also told the home health aide that she wanted to go home. I immediately went to Stacy's house when I received the call from the aide. I took Mom's blood pressure and blood sugar. Both were okay. The spell passed, and I took Mom home to rest.

Late that afternoon, Mom had another spell, and it was pretty bad. Her blood pressure was up to 224/93, and her blood sugar was 119. I called 911, and Mom was taken to McLeod Hospital Emergency Room. I also called Stacy, and she was there in minutes. Stacy and I followed the ambulance. Mom was seen by one of the staff doctors. They did a CAT scan, blood work, EKG, and urine specimen. Her blood pressure after reaching the hospital was 212/126. They gave her some blood pressure medication, and her pressure came down. The doctor said the test results were all normal. The doctor said Mom probably had a transient ischemic attack (TIA) and sent her home on her same medication. We were at the hospital for five hours. Mom went straight to bed as soon as she ate. She rested well the entire night.

April 30, 2010

I took George to his medical appointment with his primary physician early this morning. He told George that he shouldn't drive, and if he did, he would report him to the Department of Motor Vehicles. George told the doctor that he hadn't been driving at all, which was not true. George had been driving to Stacy's house, to the store, and to the dump. He actually told Gloria that he would keep driving as long as he had his license.

Dollie's Diary

***

May 1, 2010–May 31, 2010

This month started out with Mom having more and more spells. Although the spells left her within a few minutes, she was drained and very weak afterward. Mom's blood pressure was still going up and down. The doctor couldn't seem to regulate it. Her medication had been changed so many times, but nothing seemed to work. At least Mom's sugar was okay. Mom kept telling me day after day that it wouldn't be long. I sat with her in her room more and more each day now because she was not coming to the table as much. Before she started feeling so weak, we ate dinner together every day, and we had long conversations about everything. I enjoyed our talks and so did she. Since I am not a breakfast person, George or the home health aide always sat with her when she had her breakfast.

Stacy was also coming more often during the day to check on Mom and to spend time with her. At times Mom's speech was distorted or mumbled. Although we understood what she was saying, it was clear to us that something was going on. Mom complained about not being able to turn one of her hearing aids up or down. Since the knob was never replaced, Stacy drove all the way to Hartsville to drop it off for repairs. They had to send it back to the factory. We explained to Mom that she would only have one hearing aid for a couple of weeks. She said she understood.

Since Mom's health was up and down and her spells were more frequent, I told Stacy and Samuel that I was going to call Tracy and Gloria to let them know what Mom was saying. Gloria was scheduled to come home in July. I didn't know exactly when Tracy was coming. I called Tracy and Gloria and told them that Mom had been talking more and more about her time not being long. I wanted them to know that Mom was getting weaker and weaker by the day. None of us knew what God's plan was, but just in case the Lord had shown Mom something, it might be a good idea if they came home to spend some quality time with her while she was still lucid. I did not want to say they had to come because Mom could live another ten or more years. We all know that God is in control of life and death. I tried to be like Samuel when he was taking care of Mom alone. He told us how Mom was doing health wise and allowed us to make up our own minds about whether we should come or not.

We had all the prayer warriors praying for Mom, and we know that God hears and answers prayer. One of the pastors in Connecticut prophesied that Mom would recover and live another few years. We all wanted that to be true, but when you keep hearing someone say over and over again that their time is drawing near, you start believing that they must know something you don't know.

May 1, 2010

Mom seemed to be getting weaker and weaker. At times it was hard to tell how sick she was because she tried to keep things from us. I spent some time with her this morning and told her that she needs to tell me the truth about how she was feeling. She looked at me and said, "Dollie—I am not feeling well at all. It is not going to be long. You and Stacy need to hear what I'm saying—my time isn't long." I told Mom that we heard her, and we believed her, but while she was here, we were going to take good care of her. I talked to Stacy and Carnel about what Mom said this morning. Carnel reminded us of what he had been saying for week, "You better listen to what your mother is saying because she may know something that you don't know."

May 2, 2010

George and I went to church at St. Beulah today. The home health aide stayed with Mom. I spent all afternoon with Mom. Stacy also came over and watched television with her. She ate in her room because she felt weak.

May 9, 2010

George and I went to church at St. Beulah this morning. The combined choir sang. We were still having service in the Fellowship Hall. I was worried about Mom. She said she felt good, but she was so weak—and believe me, she was weak. Stacy and I spent time with her today. I told Stacy that Mom looked weak in her eyes. She could barely walk. Stacy stayed most of the afternoon and watched Rev. Patterson with her today on TV.

We both put Mom to bed and made sure she had ice water and snacks if she got hungry.

Chapter 12

***

Mom's Second Hospitalization

"To every thing there is a season, and a time to every purpose under the heaven: A time to be born, and a time to die; a time to plant, and a time to pluck up that which is planted; A time to kill, and a time to heal; a time to break down, and a time to build up; A time to weep, and a time to laugh; a time to mourn, and a time to dance."
—Ecclesiastes 3:1-4

May 13, 2010

I was so worried about Mom. She had been having spells for months, but now they were becoming more persistent and had significant outcomes. These spells were lasting longer and completely knocking her off her feet. She was not bouncing back like before. When she had a spell, she would rest for a while, and the spell would pass. In the last months, Mom's physical condition had worsened. She had been living with me for fourteen months now. During that time she had several strokes, numerous spells, bronchitis, pneumonia, end-stage Parkinson disease, congestive heart failure, an enlarged heart, and other ailments.

This morning, she had another spell, and this one was pretty bad. Mom told me, "Dollie, I'm sick—take me to the hospital and leave me there." I told Mom that I would take her to the hospital, but I couldn't just leave her there. I called 911. Mom was extremely weak. She said she was zoning in and out. Her blood pressure was 203/84, and her blood sugar was 101. I called Stacy and told her to come to the house immediately, as Mom was sick. Stacy was there within minutes. The ambulance also came very quickly and transported Mom to McLeod Hospital.

Mom looked like she was having a stroke. She was very sick and extremely weak. It took two men to get her on the stretcher because she could not help them at all. I grabbed my book, and we followed the ambulance. When we reached the hospital, I went in with Mom and Stacy waited in the waiting room. I also called Samuel and told him that Mom was sick and was being taken to the hospital. Mom's blood pressure continued to be unstable. Different hospital doctors came in and checked Mom. They did X-rays, a CAT scan, blood work, an EKG, and a urine test. Finally the doctor came in and said all the tests were normal, but they were very concerned about her elevated blood pressure. He asked for additional information on Mom, which I provided. I told the doctor about all the tests Mom had at McLeod and about her recent strokes, pneumonia, and bronchitis. I also told him that Mom might have had another stroke because the symptoms were the same as before. He said that Mom had a sinus infection. We knew that already. We also knew that her blood pressure was up and down for months and not any of her medical providers could stabilize it. The doctor said they would hospitalize her and run some more tests (i.e., MRI, CPK, etc.). Samuel later arrived and stayed until they made the decision to admit her. He then left to take care of some business. Stacy and I stayed with Mom until she was placed in her room. They put her on the third floor in the stroke unit.

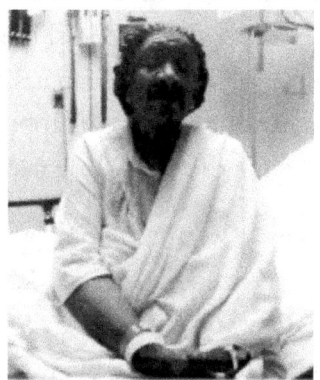

Mom after arriving at the hospital on May 13, 2010. She is still in the emergency room wearing her nightgown and head cap.

May 14, 2010–May 16, 2010

Mom remained hospitalized in the stoke unit. She seemed to be doing okay, but her blood pressure was still unstable. The doctor ordered a number of tests, and the MRI showed that Mom had suffered another stroke within the last week. The doctor said that this stroke affected a different part of her brain that had something to do with her balance and caused the weakness. At least we know now why she was so weak. Mom will need ongoing care. Mom had started physical therapy already, and she was totally exhausted when she returned to the room. We thought the physical therapist was having Mom walk too far, but learned that Mom was only walking to the desk and back, which was only a few steps outside her door. The doctor and therapist were both recommending a nursing home for Mom because she needed skilled nursing care. The hospital social worker had been assigned to Mom's case, and she was trying to find an appropriate nursing home that can provide the care Mom needs.

The family never wanted Mom to go to a nursing home, but now we realized that she needed more care than we can provide. Stacy and I were initially looking into an assisted living program for Mom, but now that was totally out of the question. Mom's home health aide recommended Commander Nursing Home, so Stacy and I went there and took a tour. It was really nice, and we both liked it. We knew that if we had to send Mom to a nursing home, we wanted the best. We knew once we found a home, we had to be visible. The social worker checked Commander, but they had no beds. She also checked Southland Nursing Home, but there were no beds available there either.

Miss Bell and Victoria came to see Mom this week at the hospital. Victoria said Mom told her and Miss Bell that her time wasn't long, as the Lord will be calling her home soon. Mom continued to believe that her time was real close at hand. She told me often that she would be leaving us soon. Mom told Miss Bell and Victoria that she was going into a nursing home because she was not well. Mom was well aware that she was very sick and needed ongoing medical care. Mom also told Miss Bell that she needed to go into a nursing home, too. At one time, Miss Bell told Mom that she was going to sign herself into a nursing home, but she never did. Victoria said the visit went well, and Mom seemed to enjoy seeing them both. The next day we asked Mom how her visit went with Victoria and Miss Bell the night before, Mom said, "They didn't come see me last night." She never remembered them being at the hospital at all.

May 17, 2010

Mom remains in the stroke unit at the hospital. When her doctor came in this morning, Mom asked him what was wrong with her. The doctor told Mom that she had another stroke recently, which had affected her balance.

The stroke also caused weakness and dehydration. When we asked about Mom's spells, he said that the spells were called absence attacks. I also asked if Mom could have another viral infection, and he said he would check that out. He ordered a brain wave test to make sure Mom was not having seizures. Mom was so weak that she needed help with everything. She was still very dizzy and lightheaded. Mom knew that the hospital was recommending a nursing home and said she agreed with their recommendation. Mom was put on potassium with sodium to help clear up her lungs. The doctor said Mom's sugar was not a concern and the medication she was taking was okay.

May 18, 2010

The hospital social worker was still looking for a nursing home for Mom. Commander and Southland are both full. The social worker was now checking Heritage and Honoridge. She said she would call them and get back to us. Mom going to a nursing home was difficult for us, as we never wanted our mother in a nursing home. However, her health had deteriorated so much that she needed full-time clinical services. The doctors were unable to stabilized her high blood pressure and she was at risk of having another stroke.

The nurses reported that Mom was being a little hardheaded and not listening. That's our Mom—she never listened to us either. The nurses said Mom was getting out of bed without assistance and going to the bathroom without alerting anyone for help. When I talked to Mom about it, she said she called them, but nobody came. She said she would wet the bed if she waited. I talked to the nurses about Mom's needs, and they said Mom sometimes presses the wrong button and thinks she has called them. Stacy and I showed Mom the button to push when she needed the nurses. We also told the nurses to please listen for her call and respond as quickly as they can. The nursing staff was very nice. They said they would listen and respond immediately when Mom called. I told Mom to call them before she had to go to the bathroom, and she said she would.

May 19, 2010

I was at the hospital with Mom today and received a call from the hospital social worker. She said she found a bed at Heritage Nursing Home, and one of their nurses wanted to come to see Mom and me that afternoon at the hospital. I told her that I would be at the hospital all day. The Heritage nurse came around lunchtime and talked with me about Mom and the nursing home. It was difficult for me to talk about sending Mom to Heritage. I was so upset that I broke down a few times. Because of Mom's current condition, she would need to have her medication administered by the nurses. I was glad to hear that all the services Mom would need were in-house (i.e. doctor, nurses, wound treatment, therapy, labs, x-rays, etc.), which were very good. She wanted to meet Mom, but Mom slept through the entire meeting. The nurse said she would let us know if they would accept Mom.

When Mom woke up, I talked with her one-on-one about everything. We talked about the hospital's recommendation and the Heritage Nursing Home. I wanted to be sure Mom understood what was going on. I told her that right now, she needed a real nursing staff to take care of her. Although I did my best, I was not a nurse. I wanted her to know that we were not trying to get rid of her. I let her know that we would do anything to keep her around as long as we can. We loved her, and we would always be there for her. I wanted to make sure she knew that she would never be abandoned and left alone. I knew Stacy also had a difficult time with this because we always talked about being there for Mom. I wanted Mom to know that we all loved her and wanted only the best for her. Mom said she understood, but I wondered in my mind if she really did. She must have known what I was thinking because she said, "Dollie, I know I'm sick, and I know I can't go home right now. You have to stop worrying so much about me. You have been good to me. I will be all right." I felt tears in my eyes, but I didn't want Mom to see me crying. The doctors had said that they did not know how long it would take Mom's strength to return or if it would. Mom's health seemed to be deteriorating on a daily basis, and her blood pressure was still so unstable. I had been worried about Mom's blood pressure for months, knowing she could have another stroke anytime. I knew the nursing home was in Mom's best interests, but it was hard. I told Mom, "What I did, I wanted to do—you are very special to me, and I love you." Mom said, "I love you, too, hon."

I stayed with Mom the remainder of the day. While she rested, I sent a text message to everyone bringing each person up-to-date on Mom's condition and latest developments. After Mom had her dinner and was out for the night, I left the hospital.

May 20, 2010

Stacy was at the hospital this morning while I went to Heritage House. Stacy called me to let me know that two of Samuel's children came to see Mom this morning. Mom was so happy to see them. However, as soon as she saw them, she had one of her spells. Stacy said Mom went into some kind of trance, what she calls zoning out. The nurse was there and for the first time saw one of Mom's spells. Stacy was happy that they finally knew what we were talking about. Stacy said she had Samuel's children leave the room while they brought Mom back. The spells last for a few minutes. After Mom came back, Stacy went out of the room to talk with Samuel's children.

I had a meeting with Heritage this morning. The intake supervisor went over the paperwork and gave me a tour of the facility. She showed me Mom's room if we accepted the placement. I signed the papers and returned to the hospital. When I arrived at the hospital, Stacy was standing outside of Mom's room talking with Samuel's children. Stacy explained what happened with Mom. Because of Mom's condition, visitors had to be restricted.

May 21, 2010–May 23, 2010

Mom was extremely weak and hardly able to do anything for herself. Her blood pressure continued to be very unstable. The doctors want to keep Mom in the hospital until they were able to get her blood pressure under control. The doctors said she needed ongoing medical care around the clock. They were still recommending a nursing home. Although we didn't want Mom to go to a nursing home, we knew that in her current condition, the doctors were right. We were not able to provide the care that Mom needed at home. Stacy and I told the social worker that we would accept the room.

Since we expected Mom to be released soon, we wanted to fix up her room as soon as possible. We worked hard that week, going back and forth from the hospital to the nursing home until everything was in place and ready for her arrival. I even took pictures to show her the room and that pleased her very much.

May 24, 2010

Mom was still hospitalized at McLeod. Stacy was at the hospital today, and I was at the nursing home. Stacy called me and said that Mom was very sick. I immediately left the nursing home and went to the hospital. When I arrived, Mom was pretty bad. Mom had been throwing up all morning. The nurse said it started very early. I told Stacy that she also threw up the day before when I was at the hospital. It was also brown fluid with specs in it. The doctors had prescribed several things, but nothing seemed to work. Mom was disoriented, reaching for objects that were not there. Her speech was distorted, and she kept throwing up. They kept giving her something for the nausea, but nothing helped. The doctor finally arrived, and we told him all Mom's symptoms. He checked Mom and wrote orders for her to have X-rays of her stomach, CAT scan, and blood work. I didn't know what to think. I thought, *"What is going on? Does she have cancer?"* I was hoping she wasn't having another stroke. I asked the doctor to check for another stroke, and he said he would. The doctor ordered something else for the nausea and something to help her sleep. We stayed with Mom until the medication took effect, and she fell asleep, then we went home for the night.

So much was happening that I forgot my son's birthday was today. Happy birthday, JR.

Chapter 13

***

Mom's Surgery

"And the prayer of faith shall save the sick, and the Lord shall raise him up; and if he have committed sins, they shall be forgiven him." — **James 5:15**

May 25, 2010

I received a call from the hospital around 6:00 A.M. stating that Mom's stomach X-rays showed that she had a small blockage in one of her intestines. They wanted me to come to the hospital right away to sign the permission form for Mom to have surgery. I jumped out of bed and left for the hospital within minutes. When I arrived at the hospital, I met with the nurse and she brought me up-to-date on the tests and their findings. I looked in on Mom, and she was asleep. The nurse said that Mom had a difficult night. They had to keep giving her something for her stomach. Mom had to be restrained, as she pulled the IV out of her arm three times during the night. I thought, *"Why did they wait until she pulled the IV out three times before they restrained her? She should have been watched after pulling it out once."* I felt so bad for Mom. I signed the permission slip and went back into Mom's room and sat with her. Since Mom was so uncomfortable when she was awake, I asked them to keep her sedated as much as possible. Mom slept all day.

The nurse said that the doctor wanted to meet with the family to explain the procedure. I called Stacy and Samuel regarding the surgery, and they both came to the hospital. The doctor was unable to meet with us before the surgery, but he called and spent time on the phone going over the procedure. Mom had surgery late that afternoon. Stacy, Samuel, and I stayed at the hospital all day. We went with Mom to the prep room before surgery. When they took Mom into surgery, we went to the waiting area.

After surgery, we met with the surgeon. He said the surgery went well, but Mom was still on the ventilator. She was in the trauma surgical care unit (TSCU), which was a sixteen-bed intensive care unit on the ninth floor of the McLeod Pavilion. The surgeon said they would try to wean her off the ventilator in three to four days. We all went up to the floor where Mom was, but Stacy said she couldn't see Mom with the breathing tube and all the other gadgets to which she was hooked up. Samuel said he couldn't take the tubes and gadgets either, but since he was sick with something, I didn't think he should be around

Mom anyway. I thought about me not being able to take the spit and the vomit, and now Stacy couldn't take the breathing tubes and machines. We complemented each other well, and Mom benefited because she had someone there through it all. I went in to see Mom in TSCU. She was hooked up to many machines, and it was difficult seeing her on the breathing machine, but I forced myself. The nurse was nice enough to explain all the machines to me. Mom looked peaceful. The nurse said Mom would be out all night. I gave her my phone numbers in case she needed me and we left for the night.

May 26, 2010

It was the day after surgery. Mom had been on the ventilator since yesterday. They kept her sedated all night, which was good. I arrived at the hospital before 6:00 A.M. She didn't know I was there. Stacy and Samuel were at home today, as they could not stand seeing Mom on all the machines. The nurses said she rested through the night. She did look peaceful. Her arms were still swollen, and there were many needles. They put a new IV in the main artery near the heart. Yes, another needle. I was told by the doctor that she would be kept on the ventilator and sedated all day. However, they would try to wean her off the ventilator in the morning. I called Stacy and gave her an update. I also called Mom's sister Victoria and told her to tell Mom's stepmother, Miss Bell, Mom's brother James, and his wife, Frances, about Mom's condition.

May 27, 2010

This was day three on the ventilator—two days after surgery. I woke up at 4:30 A.M. I didn't sleep very well last night. I was very nervous and anxious—I didn't know why. I received many calls from Chesterfield last night. They were asking about Mom. It was amazing how certain news travelled so fast; I had only called one person in Chesterfield. I did tell her to tell anyone she thought should know. Where were all these people the last sixteen months, when she was able to see or hear them? I told everyone that Mom couldn't have visitors because she was in the ICU and her immune system was still very weak. Some of the people thought I was trying to keep Mom from them, but I couldn't help what they thought. It was not about them. It was about Mom.

Carnel was mowing my lawn this morning when I walked out of the house to go to the hospital. I stopped to say hello and out of nowhere, I broke down and started crying big time. Where did that come from? I couldn't even speak—tears rolled down my face while he waited patiently to see if something happened to Mom. I told him, "Nothing happened. I'm just a little stressed." I got in my car, composed myself, and drove to the hospital.

I arrived at the hospital a little before 8:00 A.M., found a parking space, and went up to Mom's room. She was on the ninth floor in TSCU, room fifteen. I met with Mom's nurse and the doctor. They started weaning Mom off the ventilator around 8:15 A.M. She started waking up. She was very uncomfortable. Tears rolls down her face. I let her know I was there but received no response. I stood by her bed, rubbing her hands. She looked at me but was unable to speak. The doctor told me, "Your job is to keep her awake—talk to her—stimulate her. I thought, *"Easier said than done. How do you stimulate someone who is uncomfortable and in so much pain?"* I could see how uncomfortable Mom was. Her entire body was swollen. I thought, *"Oh my God, how much more?"* She was hooked up to so many machines. She had to tolerate that breathing tube an hour or more (wide awake) for them to take it out. I felt so bad for her. I hated seeing my mother suffer, and she was suffering. All of a sudden, she looked at me as if she just recognized who I was. You could feel her excitement, as she started to lift her head in an effort to try and talk to me, but she couldn't. I told her to lie still. I calmed her down and said, "Mom, we are here." She realized she was not alone, and she calmed down.

They took blood at 9:22 A.M. to see if she was tolerating breathing on her own. I prayed, "Lord, have mercy." She looked so helpless. I asked how long we had to wait before they knew if it could be removed. The nurse said they would know quickly if the tube could come out. A few minutes felt like an hour. The nurse said the numbers were not good. Her blood pressure was very high, and she had lots of fluid in her lungs. Mom was breathing on her own, but the doctor was concerned that she would not breathe deep enough to get rid of the fluid in her lungs. He wanted to keep her on the machine another day and try again tomorrow. I thought, *"I don't believe she has to go through this again tomorrow."* The nurse gave Mom a breathing treatment, a shot in her stomach to keep her from getting blood clots, meds for her high blood pressure, and sedation meds to help her rest and be more comfortable. The doctor said the signs were fairly good today, but he wanted to make sure before they took her off. She was considered borderline right now. He did not want to put the tube back in if she was not able to breathe on her own. I thought, *"Oh no—they won't put it back in if they take it out."* Mom was so uncomfortable that I was glad when they put her back to sleep. She calmed down and seemed so relaxed. I called Stacy and gave her an update.

May 28, 2010

It had been three days since Mom's surgery, which was day four on the ventilator. Mom was given water pills and Lasix for the fluid buildup. She was so swollen, even more than yesterday. I arrived early this morning. They started trying to wean Mom off the ventilator at 8:00 A.M. this morning. She was much calmer through the trial today.

I tried talking to Mom, but she did not respond today. I asked the nurse about her lack of response, and she told me they gave her morphine to help keep her calm. What? Why didn't they give it to her yesterday? Mom was so uncomfortable yesterday that tears were running down her face. She looked at me as to say, "Why are you letting them do this to me?" My heart was broken seeing her go through that without any pain medication. I didn't know she could have morphine during the weaning. I hated it that Mom had to go through that yesterday, but I was happy she had something today. The blood pressure shot up again during the weaning. I spoke to her doctor, and he said he wanted to keep her on the ventilator another day, as she was still not where they wanted her to be. Mom was sedated again and soon looked as though she was sleeping. They would try to wean her again tomorrow. I wondered how much more Mom could take, as the weaning was difficult for her. I also wondered how much more I could take seeing her go through it all. This was very difficult for me. The nurses seemed to be very good with Mom. They removed the two IVs that were in her hand. Mom would have a long road back, as she was a very sick lady. I called Stacy to give her an update.

I stayed at the hospital all day. I knew Mom was sedated and didn't know I was there, but I stayed anyway. I spoke to the nurse at 4:15 P.M. to see if she knew when the doctors were coming. As soon as I left the desk, Mom's doctors came by. I asked them how Mom was really doing.

The doctors wanted Mom to get a little dryer (fluids), so they gave her more Lasix today. They were not pleased with Mom's blood pressure, her lungs, her urine output, or her heart rate. He said her vital signs were otherwise good. They identified so many bad things that I almost felt defeated. I had to remind myself that God was still in control of this situation. I closed my eyes and asked the Lord for strength, as I was exhausted. I also asked him to have mercy on Mom. The doctor said they would try to wean her off the ventilator again tomorrow morning around 8:00 A.M. I left the hospital to get a little rest because I wanted to be there early in the morning before they woke Mom up for the weaning.

May 29, 2010

This was Mom's fifth day on the ventilator—four days after her surgery. I stopped by Stacy's house on my way to the hospital this morning. I was so upset all afternoon yesterday after leaving the hospital that I didn't sleep at all last night. I thought of Mom's face and eyes looking up at me as if to say, "Why are you letting them do this to me?" I honestly felt she was thinking that. I felt so helpless. I thought, "*I hope she understands that the only thing I can do for her is to be there with her and pray.*" Watching Mom go through this was even more distressing to me because this was my third go round. My husband, George, and my daughter, Latisha, both had aneurysms and were on breathing tubes after their surgeries. Here I was again, seeing those begging eyes asking for help and there was nothing I could do but pray. I prayed and asked God again for mercy.

"If ye shall ask anything in My name, I will do it." —John 14:14 (KJV)

When I got to the hospital, there were lots of parking spaces. I thought for a minute—it was Saturday. It's funny how stress makes you lose track of time and everything else. I was stressed out of my mind, sleeping only about two to three hours a night. I was probably running on an empty tank.

When I reached Mom's room, she was sleeping—still quite swollen but not as much as the day before. She looked good, if you overlooked the tubes, IVs, and other gadgets she was hooked up to. I checked her out from her head to her toes. I had been taking pictures daily to see if there were any visible changes. There were none yet. I stood there and watched her sleep. Her skin was so smooth, as Mom always took care of her skin. Even the nurses complimented her skin. She always bought special creams for her face, and it was obvious they worked. My mother was always a very beautiful woman.

The nurse came in and said she was going to cut the sedation (Propofal) meds off and start the weaning. I closed my eyes and said, "Lord have mercy." This was the part

I hated. Seeing Mom uncomfortable was something that I never wanted to see again, but I had to be there for her, even if I could not do anything to ease her discomfort. At least she knew I was there. I asked them to give her some pain medication because she had done better yesterday with the morphine. The nurse said she would try some. Thank God, I got to the hospital in time, as she was going to wean her without medication. The first day was awful for Mom without pain meds. She cried through the pain.

In the beginning of the weaning, Mom was extremely uncomfortable. I reminded the nurse about the morphine, but she did not give it to her. I thought, *"If they know she is in pain, why do I have to tell them to give her pain medication?"* I knew it was a different nurse, so I told her what they did the day before, but she said the doctor wanted to see how Mom did on her own. He did not prescribe any morphine for this morning. I said, "What? Why didn't you tell me that before when I mentioned the morphine earlier?" I fought back the tears, trying to stay strong for Mom. She was trying to get that tube out, so I held her hands down to keep her from pulling the tube out. This was almost impossible, as Mom was strong and wanted that tube out. I kept insisting that they give Mom the pain medication until I couldn't take it anymore. At that time, I reminded myself of my sister Stacy when she got upset, I enunciated every syllable, "Give her the morphine." I was so angry that I wanted to fight that nurse. She knew I was upset, and I wasn't going to back down. I honestly felt that I scared the nurse because she walked out of the room and brought back some morphine and gave Mom a small dose. Mom immediately calmed down but still appeared very uncomfortable. They did an echocardiogram to check out her heart. Her blood pressure went up to 238/115. Out of nowhere I started singing to Mom. I began to sing, "Jesus keeps me near the cross", and "Oh it is Jesus." Mom just looked at me, almost like she wanted to help me sing. My heart was overflowing, and I fought back the tears. I could feel my voice shaking, and I could see tears rolling down Mom's face. I felt so bad for her.

They gave her two more blood pressure meds and Lasik for the fluid. The nurse questioned me about a living will. I told them that Mom didn't have one, but the family knew her wishes. She would not want to go through this. I told her that Mom wanted the tube out now. For the first time, Mom shook her head in agreement. I was shocked and happy that Mom responded. The nurse said, "It's pretty clear that's what she wants." That's when the tears welled up in my eyes and ran down my cheeks. I turned and wiped my face, so Mom would not see me cry. When I looked at Mom, tears were running down her face, too. She finally got the nurses to understand what she wanted—yes, she made a decision. Mom was able to tell them herself that she wanted the tubes out.

I felt good because I knew at that moment that Mom knew I was there advocating for her. She was not alone.

The nurse asked me, "If we take it out, and it doesn't work, what then?" I told the nurse that if they take the tube out, and it doesn't work, Mom would not want them to put it back in. I told the nurse that we have given this to God. Whatever His will was, we would accept. Mom was sick, and she has suffered enough. Looking at her at that moment, I knew for a fact that she did not want that. Mom always told me, "I have lived my life. Don't cry over me because I have made peace with God." My mother did have a good life. Her last years were good years. She was very happy. I looked toward heaven and prayed for peace, joy and everlasting life. No more pain or sorrow—just happiness for my mom.

They took the breathing tube out. At first, Mom had some difficulty breathing, but they gave her oxygen, morphine, and antibiotics to help with the infection. I called Stacy to let her know the breathing tube was out. She later came to the hospital. At 2:40 P.M., the doctor came in to speak with us. He said Mom was holding her own, but it could go either way. Her lungs had become weak because of her age. If it were his mother, he would not put her through that again. We agreed, as it was our mother, and we would not allow them to put that tube back down her throat. Mom tried to talk to Stacy and me, but it was extremely difficult to understand what she was saying. We got some of it but not all. Stacy became very upset at times when she could not understand Mom. In fact, it was hard for both of us because we knew Mom was desperately trying to tell us something.

Sunday, May 30, 2010

After Mom was taken off the ventilator, Stacy and I decided to take turns at the hospital because we were both drained. Today was Stacy's day at the hospital, but she woke up with some kind of virus, and we thought it would be better for her not to be around Mom at that time. I went to the hospital and stayed with Mom today. I got there before 6:00 A.M., as I wanted to be there before she woke up. Mom was still asleep. I checked her from her head to her toes as usual. She was still quite swollen. She was breathing very hard this morning, as if every breath was her last. I stood over her and watched her for a while. She was so sick, and I couldn't do anything about it. Mom was still nonresponsive today. I tried talking to her, singing to her, and even reading the Bible to her, but she did not respond to anything. I sat there all morning, watching TV, and reading the newspaper.

All of a sudden, the machines started beeping very loudly. I jumped up to see what was going on. The nurses' station was right outside Mom's door and one of the nurses motioned to me, "I'm on it." She appeared to be reading Mom's electronic EKG. All at once, several nurses came into the room and started working on Mom. Mom was still sleeping as though nothing was happening. They started giving Mom some nitroglycerin, potassium, magnesium, and an aspirin suppository. Another nurse had a portable EKG machine and hooked Mom up for an EKG. A heart specialist from Pee Dee Cardiology Associates came in and said Mom had a heart attack. Mom slept through it all. She did not respond to anyone, other than shaking her head yes or no when they got her to open her eyes. Mom was still very sick.

I called Stacy and Samuel and told them that Mom had a heart attack. They both came to the hospital. Mom continued to be nonresponsive. They turned her at 5:30 P.M., but she did not indicate that she knew she was moved. We left the hospital a little after 6:00 P.M. I called back later, and Mom was still resting. They gave her a bath and changed her clothes. Nurse Howard said she had a good night.

May 31, 2010

I was at the hospital at 7:35 A.M. this morning. I wanted to catch her doctors, as we kept missing each other. Mom was still on nitroglycerin and potassium. She was also being fed through her IV. She was off 100 percent oxygen and was now on 99 percent. The swelling had gone down some, but parts of her body were still swollen. They put a larger waistband on, so Mom could breathe better. She was still in TSCU. They were going to try to get her up in a chair today. They would use a lift machine to get her out of bed and into the chair. I was very tired today. My back was pretty bad, and I got no sleep last night. Hopefully, when Mom started feeling better, I would deal with my back issues.

Respiratory gave Mom a treatment at 8:40 A.M. Mom was still experiencing some difficulty breathing. She needed to cough, as she was very congested. When Mom woke up, she looked at me. She appeared very weak. I asked if she knew who I was. She said, "Yes, you are Dollie—my Dollie." Mom appeared to be happy to see me, and I was happy to see her awake and in her right mind. Mom just looked at me and smiled. That made me feel good. She tried desperately to talk to me this morning, but I couldn't understand some of what she was saying. I asked if she was in pain, and she said no. I felt so bad when I couldn't understand her. I almost broke down at her bed this morning, but I knew I had to be strong for her. I couldn't let her see me weak.

The heart doctor said her heart function had gotten better, but she was on a nitroglycerin patch. She had been hospitalized since May 13, nineteen days ago. She was still heavily sedated, and her speech remained distorted. At times, we couldn't understand a word she was saying. We were told that Mom's prognosis was guarded. It could go either way. They were giving her so much medication to keep her from having a stroke or a heart attack that I wondered what would happen when they start weaning her off everything? Mom had a long way to go.

The nurse suctioned Mom's mouth out and got a lot of blood in the tube. Mom was coughing up blood. This looked bad. I tried to wipe Mom's mouth out whenever she would let me, as she did not want anyone going near her mouth.

Mom's doctor came in. She said that Mom was critically ill and her prognosis was guarded. Mom had a bad bacterial infection (pseudomonas) in one of her lungs. She was given antibiotic for seven days, but it did not kill the bacteria. She would be starting Mom on a stronger antibiotic to kill the bacteria. She said Mom was still at high risk. The surgery site was much improved. However, her respiratory status was most concerning, as it looked and sounded worse today. She had a heart attack on May 30 and now this bacteria. She was receiving nutrition through her IV. Her diabetes was in an uncontrolled status, but they gave her insulin at bedtime.

The heart and pulmonary doctors came in. They started the new antibiotics at 12:15 P.M. Mom now had pneumonia.

Even though it wasn't Stacy's day, she showed up in the early afternoon and also brought me lunch. Mom recognized her right away. Mom asked Stacy where Tracy and Gloria were. Mom said, "They didn't come. They didn't come." Stacy looked at me and said, "She is worried about her children." We told Mom that she needed to rest and not to worry about anything. Everybody was fine. We told her that her family members from Chesterfield were calling to see how she was doing. We talked with Mom's pastor and two other ministers from her church. They were all praying for her. We told Mom that she was loved by a lot of people. We always told her that we loved her, but we made a special point today to let her know how much. We kept telling her that we loved her. Mom said over and over again, "I love you, too. I love all of you so much." She fell asleep telling us that she loved us.

June 1, 2010

Stacy stayed at the hospital today with Mom. The doctor told Stacy that Mom was no better, but she was no worse either. She was breathing better than three days ago. She was still very weak and somewhat swollen, especially her legs. They moved her to the step-down unit today. Stacy said she slept through the move. She was still having those dreams—going way back in the past. Stacy gave me the telephone numbers and the name of Mom's night nurse in the step-down unit, so I could call to check on Mom during the night.

Stacy had a difficult day with Mom at the hospital. She said Mom moaned and groaned all day. She was in so much pain, and we could do nothing about it but pray. Stacy called me crying today. She said, "I don't know how long I can watch Mom suffer like this." We cried together on the phone, as I felt the same way. It was my day tomorrow, and it was beginning to get to me as well.

> Lead me to the rock that is higher than I
> Lead me to the rock that is higher than I
> He is my joy, my strength
> He is my all, and all and all
> Lead me, lead me and I will follow thee
> If you follow Jesus
> You will find power, love, peace and happiness
> If you follow Jesus
> He will give you joy inside
> Ask and it shall be given
> Seek and ye shall find
> If you follow Jesus
> You will find peace of mind
> Lord if you lead me, lead me and I will follow thee.
>
> —written by my sister Stacy

June 2, 2010

It was my day at the hospital with Mom. I arrived before 7:00 A.M. Mom was sleeping. She was moaning and asking the Lord to have mercy. I asked the nurse when she last had pain medication, and she said 6:00 A.M. She still had that bad rattle in her throat. The pulmonary nurse came in around 8:15 A.M. to give Mom a treatment. Mom refused to open her mouth to let her suction the mucus out. The nurse tried to force it, but I stopped her. I told the nurse that I would get it out. We did not want anyone to force our mother to do anything else. I knew Mom needed to cough and get it out, but enough is enough. Mom would fight them and cry when they tried to stick that suction tube down her throat. I told Mom to calm down because we would not let them do that again. Mom looked at me and immediately calmed down. She went back to sleep.

All of a sudden Mom called out my name very loudly. "Dollie." I jumped up because she was very clear. I went to her bedside and asked if she was all right. She said, "I'm all right. How are you doing? Are you getting any rest?" I told her I was doing well. She said, "Dollie, I'm sorry I got sick. I know you are tired and can't get any rest." It was clear that Mom was worried about me. I kept telling her that I was all right. I told her that I was not taking care of her alone. Stacy and I had been taking turns at the hospital with her. I told her that she was not alone. I told her not to worry because we were going to take good care of her. She said, "All right." As soon as she saw that I was all right, she went back to sleep. I also told her that she had to cough for me when she woke up, so that we could get that mucus out. She said all right and went back to sleep.

The heart nurse came in and checked Mom. She said that the heart doctor would be in later. Mom's legs are still swollen and very sore. The heart doctor came in and checked Mom. He said her heart was doing well. They would keep an eye on that. He heard some movement in her bowels—felt like they were beginning to wake up. I felt good about that because the bowels were supposed to wake up about three to four days after surgery. I asked about liquids because Mom had been asking for water. He said that the surgeon would decide when she could take some liquids. He said it had taken a little longer for the bowels to wake up. The pulmonary doctor came in and said Mom's breathing was better. Although I couldn't see any change in Mom's condition, both doctors said Mom was doing better.

All the doctors and nurses had been saying that Mom was getting better. I really couldn't see it. I wanted to believe them, but Mom looked bad to me. I hated seeing her suffer. She was still very weak and was fed through her IV. She had a stroke, heart attack, and pneumonia. Her breathing still seemed hoarse to me, and she was still in so much pain. How could they say she was better? I didn't see it.

The nurses came and lifted her out of bed today. For the first time in two weeks, she was sitting up in a chair. The bad thing was that she didn't know she was in a chair. She was just that sick. Her breathing was still very rough. They wanted to stick something down her throat to get the mucus out, but we said no. Mom hated the ventilator and wanted nothing to do with invasive treatments. I was a little leery about her being taken out of bed today, but Mom seemed to tolerate the move okay. The nurse said they would let Mom stay in the chair a couple of hours. Mom slept through the entire move. After two hours, I went to get the nurse, so they could put Mom back to bed. After a while, I started getting a little heated because it seemed as though they were dragging their feet. I went to the desk and insisted that someone put Mom back in bed. This was the first time she was out of bed since the surgery. Even though she slept through it all, I didn't want her to overdo the first day.

The nurses came in apologizing for taking so long, and I told them that she had been up too long. I did not want to hear any apology; I wanted them to put Mom back to bed. They hooked Mom up to the lift and started to lift her out of the chair. Mom had a fit. She kept saying, "Lord have mercy, oh Lord." It was awful. She was in so much pain that I made them stop and give her some morphine. They had her halfway out of the chair in midair, but I would not let them move Mom another inch until they gave her some pain medication. The nurse went and got some morphine to help with the pain. Mom was still very sick and needed someone to advocate for her, and I refused to let them hurt her anymore. After they got her back in bed, I noticed that her dressing was soaking wet. The nurse removed the dressing and bloody liquid ran out of the wound. She called the surgeon immediately and asked him to come to check Mom's wound.

The surgeon came in a few minutes later to check Mom's wound. It was terrible. Even though Mom had just been given morphine, she was still in pain. The surgeon reopened the wound without giving her anything else. When he pulled some of the staples out, pus mixed with blood ran out. He said Mom had an infection, but it would be all right. They cleaned the wound with peroxide and replaced the dressing.

I felt so sorry for Mom that I could no longer control my emotions. I broke down and started crying so badly that the nurse had to console me. I told the nurse that I wanted to speak with her doctor, as Mom was suffering and did not seem to be getting any better. I wanted to know how Mom really was and I wanted to know today. The nurse mentioned the palliative care program. I told her that I have already been told about the program, but no one had come to talk with the family about it. I told the nurse that we wanted to talk with someone as soon as possible about our mother. She said she would have someone come and talk with us today or tomorrow. I kept thinking, *"Mom would not want to go through this, as she would want to maintain her dignity and respect. What kind of morphine are they giving her because she is hurting all the time? We wanted her comfortable. Not later, but now."*

I stayed at the hospital all day. I made sure I was by Mom's bedside when she was awake. When she slept, I used my laptop to type up my notes. I also wrote Mom a letter. When Mom felt better, I wanted to read it to her.

A Letter to My Mom
June 2, 2010

Dear Mom,

I was thinking of you today and thought that I would write you a letter. One spring day in 1945 you gave birth to me, your third child and first daughter. I often wondered what you were thinking on that day when you first heard the words "It's a girl," especially after having two hardheaded boys.

So many times we take things for granted, but we must remember that it only takes a moment for a person's life to change—in the twinkle of an eye or a mere second, your entire life as you know it can be different. Mom, you often said that you had a good life. I believe you did. You met and married Dad at an early age. You stayed at home and raised your children while Daddy worked and took care of the family. Daddy was ambitious and had a lot of dreams. For a man to achieve so much in his time was such an accomplishment. I was proud to let people know that he was my father. And Mom, I am also proud of you. I remember our many conversations about your relationship with God. You spent hours in your room praying and having what you called your private moments with the Lord. You told me that you have made peace with the Lord and that you are ready whenever He comes for you. I am so glad you spent time with God, and I truly believe that you are ready for eternal life. I know that God is still in charge. Yes, He is in total control of our lives and every situation. No, He does not make any mistakes.

Mom, I believe you were a good wife. You and Dad had your moments like any other married couple, but you stood by each other through thick and thin. A lot of people were envious of your marriage. Yes, you had a right to be proud of those wonderful years you and Dad spent together. And Mom, you are also a wonderful mother. When we were young, you were a strong disciplinarian, but you always took time to talk and play with us. The relationship you have with your children should let you know how much we love and respect you. You and Dad have inspired all of us to become responsible adults. We all love you, and we know that you love us, too. Yes, Mom, you achieved your goals, and that is something you should be very proud of.

Mom, like everyone else, I, too, had dreams—some large and some small, and some achieved and some not. You reach a point in your life where your priorities change. Things that were important are not anymore. Things that you held precious don't mean that much anymore. Things that you wanted to do become secondary. Yes, life changes. I am more focused on what is important. I thank God for His blessings. I thank God for putting me in a place where I could carry out His plan to take care of my mother. I accepted this challenge and did my best. Mom, I love you and wanted you to know what I did, I wanted to do. You are special, and I love you.

Your daughter,
Dollie

CHAPTER 14

***

A Crack in the Sky

"But He was wounded for our transgressions, He was bruised for our iniquities: the chastisement of our peace was upon him; and with his stripes we are healed." —Isaiah 53:5

June 3, 2010

Stacy stayed at the hospital all day with Mom today. Stacy said Mom was doing about the same. She was very uncomfortable. Today was very difficult for Stacy. I offered to relieve her, but she said she was okay. Gloria was scheduled to fly in from Connecticut that afternoon. She asked me to pick her up from Samuel's house in Hemingway after 6:00 P.M.

While en route to Samuel's house, I received a telephone call from Mom's doctor around 5:30 P.M. She said she wanted to call regarding Mom's condition. I stopped the car to talk with her. She said that they had been aggressive in their treatment, but there had been no change in her condition. They felt that they had done everything that they could possibly do, but it had reached a point where everything was hindering instead of helping—the treatment seemed to be causing more suffering than benefit. The doctors felt that they were not getting anywhere at that point. She said we needed to come up with an alternative plan. I asked for her honest opinion, although I know that God was in charge. Would she recover? She said that given all the treatment and the way her body had responded, it was less likely that she would recover. I felt my heart drop. It was so loud that it sounded like a crack in the sky. Tears ran down my face, and in my mind I kept saying, "God is still in charge. God is still in charge." I tried to compose myself and said to Mom's doctor that we had already put Mom in God's hands because he is the healer. The family wanted our mother to be comfortable, while her dignity and self-respect were maintained. We did not want her to be put through any intrusive treatment for nothing.

She asked if we would agree for them to take her off everything she doesn't need and possibly put her on a morphine drip, which would be more comfortable for her. She mentioned the palliative care team and hospice. I let her know that I would be talking with my siblings within the next few minutes, and I would be at the hospital all day tomorrow. I called Stacy immediately from the car and gave her the information. I also spoke with Samuel and Gloria and brought them up-to-date. Mom was still a very sick woman. Mom's doctor said she would plan a meeting with the palliative care team regarding alternative treatment for Mom.

After I picked Gloria up from Samuel's house, I took her by the hospital to see Mom. Mom was asleep when we arrived. However, she woke up when I moved her arm to place it on a pillow. She was extremely uncomfortable. Gloria got very emotional when she saw Mom. In my mind I thought about how much Mom wanted to spend time with Gloria and Tracy. I also thought about how I called them some weeks earlier about possibly coming home to spend some quality time with Mom while she was doing well. I don't know why it came to mind at that time, but it did. I did not say anything to Gloria because she was already having a hard time seeing Mom in her condition. I called the nurse and requested some pain medication for Mom. After they gave her the meds and she was asleep, we left the hospital and went home.

> **"Confess your faults one to another, and pray one for another, that ye may be healed. The effectual fervent prayer of a righteous man availeth much."**
> **—James 5:16**

June 4, 2010

It was my day to be at the hospital with Mom. I arrived at the hospital early this morning. Gloria said she would stay at the hospital today with Mom and me. Mom seemed to be doing a little better this morning. She recognized both of us and was talking nonstop for a few minutes. She asked me how I was doing. She always seems to worry about me and did not want me to get sick. She asked the nurse what was wrong with her. I told the nurse to tell her the truth. The nurse told Mom that she came in after having a stroke. She had emergency surgery, and her stomach was sore because of the stitches. She also had a heart attack. Mom said, "I want to go home." I wanted her to go home too, but Mom was in no condition to leave the hospital. I talked with Mom and asked how she was feeling. She said, "I'm sick, but I'll be all right." I told her Gloria was there and she said, "Where?" I motioned for Gloria to come to the bed, and she did. Mom called her name several times and asked how she was doing. She kept asking Gloria, "You all right? You okay?" Gloria started crying, and I told her to walk away. Mom saw her crying and told Gloria, "I'm sick, but I'm gonna be all right."

Mom was very glad to see Gloria. She asked about Tracy and Miss Bell. I told Gloria that Mom had asked about her and Tracy earlier. Mom had said, "They didn't come." I called Tracy and Miss Bell and asked them both to come see Mom today, as she was asking for them. At first Tracy said she would be there the following day, but I told Tracy she needed to come today. Tracy said she would be here as soon as she got her car fixed—sometime today. I spoke with Victoria about bringing Miss Bell to see Mom today. Victoria said she would go to her house right away and bring her to Florence. Victoria later called back and said Ms. Bell was too tired to come this morning, as she went to see her son yesterday. Victoria told me that she would bring her tomorrow. I told Victoria that she needed to come today because tomorrow was not promised.

The heart nurse and respiratory technician came in and checked Mom. Mom's bowels were still asleep. Mom was given medication for pain. Mom went back to sleep, but when she woke up that afternoon, she was very uncomfortable and did not respond to us at all.

I received a call from the Heritage Nursing Home stating they wanted us to remove Mom's stuff, as they had a resident moving into that room on Monday.

Dr. Foxen from palliative care came in and checked Mom. His bedside manner was wonderful. He also seemed to be a sensitive man, with lots of compassion. He said, "This woman is in pain and suffering. If she were my mother, I would not put her through this." He answered one of the questioned that Samuel had, "What would they do if it was their mother?" The nurse said, "Dr. Foxen is good at what he does. He cares about his patients. If anyone was called to do that job, he was." Dr. Foxen introduced himself to Gloria and me. I called Stacy and Samuel while Dr. Foxen was in the room. He met with us on the spot and explained everything to us. Dr. Foxen stated that Mom might wake up and talk with us or she might not talk at all. Samuel and Stacy were on the telephone and were able to ask Dr. Foxen questions. I was happy that at least four of us were available and in agreement.

Dr. Foxen said he wanted to get rid of all the liquids, as Mom could drown on her own fluid. She could develop shortness of breath and other things. Mom would be weaned off the liquids. They started her on a low dose of morphine every hour on a pump. They would also start her on medication to help dry her up. He said that sometimes it felt like a patient was being tortured to live longer for us.

Dr. Foxen had the nurse pull the tube out of Mom's nose. When the nurse approached Mom to pull the tube out, Mom started to fight the nurse. At that point, I was so upset that I could not even help calm Mom. Gloria stood by the bed and said that the nurse was so quick that Mom did not have a chance to fight. Mom felt her nose to see if the tube was still there. Mom relaxed after she felt it was gone.

Dr. Foxen said that he would take away everything that was not helping her. They started to wean her off the medication and all the liquids. Mom looked so much better without the tube in her nose. They started the morphine drip and gave Mom a little extra to help her relax. You could see the difference in Mom, as she was so relaxed and looked as though she was taking a nap. Dr. Foxen talked about hospice care and said he would have someone come from hospice to talk with us.

Mom's doctor came in and stated that they did not have any beds at the hospice. However, they would treat Mom as though she was already a hospice patient. That afternoon, Mom was back like she was the last two days. She was still uncomfortable, as it took time for the pain medication to get in her system. Mom was not responding to us at all. Stacy and I sang to her, and it seemed to calm her down. I also read the Bible to her. She loved Psalm 27. We stayed with Mom until the medication was in her system. Mom was very relaxed when we left the hospital. The morphine drip was working very well, and she did not appear to be in any pain at all.

"The Lord is my light and my salvation; whom shall I fear? The Lord is the strength of my life; of whom shall I be afraid? When the wicked, even mine enemies and my foes, came upon me to eat up my flesh, they stumbled and fell." — Psalm 27:1–2

After we got home, I received a call saying that Tracy was at the hospital. She said she sat with Mom in the room for a while, but Mom never woke up. I called Tracy and told her not to wake Mom up, as Mom was very uncomfortable when she was awake. I wanted Mom to be as comfortable as possible.

June 5, 2010

Tracy, Stacy, Gloria, and I were all at the hospital with Mom today. Mom rested all night. Mom's hands were still swollen. Dr. Foxen came in to check Mom at 8:45 A.M. Dr. Foxen said that Mom had chronic medical problems that had affected the functioning part of the brain. Mom had Parkinson disease, a heart attack, stroke, and pneumonia. In addition, her respiratory function was of concern. She now had end-stage Parkinson. Dr. Foxen stopped all testing, Lasix, labs, and respiratory treatment on Mom. He said he would call Peggy from McLeod Hospice House and have her come to the hospital with the paperwork.

> **"Now faith is the substance of things hoped for, the evidence of things not seen." —Hebrews 11:1**

Peggy (Hospice House) came in to talk with us. I signed all the necessary paperwork for Mom to go to the hospice. My hands were shaking, and I felt like screaming, but I forced myself to stay calm. I had to keep wiping the tears away to see where to sign. I didn't want my sisters to see how upset I was. I thought, *"What does this mean? How can I sign papers for them to take my mother to a place where most people die? I know God is able to raise her up off her sick bed, but is it His will?* I could feel myself almost breaking down, so I went into the bathroom and prayed. Stacy came in, and we talked for a few minutes. I thanked her for being so supportive through all of this, as she was there when I needed her.

Peggy said she would go check to see if any beds were available. When asked about the cost, she said that the hospice was totally free. She said that I needed to change Mom's Medicare over to Medicare hospice. I looked at Stacy and said, "We just changed it to Medicare nursing home." Within the next hour, we were informed that they had a bed for Mom at Hospice House.

Mom was moved to Hospice House late that afternoon. Mom was totally out of it during the move. We all watched the ambulance drivers to make sure they were careful with Mom. At one time Mom's arm fell off the stretcher, and I knew at that moment, we were losing her. After Mom was loaded on the stretcher and put in the ambulance, we all followed them to the facility. When we arrived at the hospice, we waited in the waiting area while they put Mom in her room. Someone came in and had me sign additional paperwork. When we entered the room, Mom was in bed still asleep. Mom looked so peaceful. She had started draining some white fluid out of her mouth. Tracy and I cleaned her mouth. We sat with Mom the remainder of the afternoon. Before leaving hospice house, I called Mom's pastor and told him that he could come see Mom.

I went to Mom's bedside and told her how much I loved her. I told her that I was going home, but Stacy, Gloria, and Tracy were still there with her. I told her that I would see her tomorrow. I was totally drained and could not hold the tears back any longer. I felt so overwhelmed and sad. I really needed to be alone. I kissed Mom good night and left the facility. That was the last time I saw Mom alive.

Chapter 15

***

Divine Peace

"But I would not have you to be ignorant, brethren, concerning them which are asleep, that ye sorrow not, even as others which have no hope. For if we believe that Jesus died and rose again, even so them also which sleep in Jesus will God bring with him." —1 Thessalonians 4:13-14

June 6, 2010

My mother passed away this morning at 7:45 A.M. This was a pretty dark day for the family. We all had today planned out. Stacy, Tracy, and Gloria were staying with Mom at hospice this morning, while I went to church. Stacy had told me last night that she wanted to have some private time with Mom, and I had asked for the same that afternoon. After church, I had planned to go to the hospice and sit with Mom while they went shopping at Roses. I had written Mom a letter, and I wanted to read it to her. She loved it when I read to her. We would spend hours going over my notes regarding her condition. She wanted me to share the notes with everyone, as she said, "People just don't know how sick I am—they need to hear what I went through."

I was sitting on the side of my bed talking to Gloria when the phone rang. I picked it up and said hello. A voice on the other end said she was calling from Hospice House regarding Mom. She went on to say that she went into the room to check on Mom and her heartbeat was somewhat weak at first but soon stopped. She stopped breathing and passed away quietly a few minutes ago. I went blank after she said, "Your mother passed away a few minutes ago." "She stopped breathing," was all I heard. Gloria took the phone, as I was in no condition to talk. I was in shock. Oh my God, my mother was gone. I cried for I don't know how long. I thought, *"We have to tell the others."* I threw something on and drove around to Stacy's house. I knew it was going to be hard telling Stacy and Tracy, but it had to be done. I walked into the house and told Stacy, Carnel, and Tracy—they were very upset. I asked the Lord to give all of us the strength we needed to get through this. I called Samuel and gave him the news. He said he would be in Florence shortly.

"Be of good courage, and He shall strengthen your heart, all ye that hope in the Lord."—Psalm 31:24

Gloria and I drove over to the hospice. Mom was still in bed—she looked very peaceful. I talked to her, touched her, and kissed her good-bye. My heart was broken—I felt so much grief. I called Stacy and Tracy to see if they wanted to come to the hospice before I had the body picked up. They said they would come. I called the funeral director and made arrangements for the funeral home to pick the body up in about an hour. This would give Stacy and Tracy time to spend with Mom.

Gloria and I met with the hospice nurse. She said Mom never woke up. Mom was not struggling at all when she passed, and she went peacefully. The hospice nurse was with her when Mom met the Lord. She said when she first entered the room, she checked Mom and heard a heartbeat. However, when she moved the stethoscope, she couldn't find a heartbeat. Her heart had stopped that quickly—she was gone.

Stacy, Tracy, and Carnel arrived. We all sat with Mom until the person from the funeral home came. The funeral director met with the family, and we told him that Mom wanted to be buried within three days. The funeral was set for Tuesday, June 8, 2010 at 1:00 P.M. We arranged to meet with the funeral director at the funeral home on Monday, June 7, at 2:00 P.M. to view and approve the remains.

June 7, 2010

The family met with the funeral director this afternoon to go over the final arrangements and to approve everything. It was pretty hard, but I tried to stay strong for my younger sisters. Stacy and Tracy were both very upset at the funeral home. They expected Mom to look more like herself than she did. Mom was very sick for a long time. I didn't like the way she looked either, but I forced myself to show no emotion and be there for them. I held everything in at the hospice and the funeral home. I kept asking the Lord for strength, and He gave me the strength I needed to get through the day. After I got home, I went to my room, closed the door, and cried until I could cry no more. My heart hurt like never before. I missed my mother so much that I could hardly stand it.

June 8, 2010

My mother was laid to rest at Grove Baptist Church today. We honored her wishes and buried her within the three-day period and did not open the casket at the church. We tried to do everything she asked us to do. Samuel spoke for the family and did an excellent job. We were all proud of him. Mom's pastor said some wonderful things about Mom, who was an active member of the church for over sixty years before she became ill and was unable to attend church services. My mother loved her pastor and Grove

Baptist Church. The pastor made it clear that he loved my mother, too.

One thing happened after the service that surprised me. Samuel and I were approached by someone stating that we disrespected his wife because she was not mentioned during the services. He said she did a lot for our mother and she should have been recognized. This was our mother's home going service. The only remarks came from the family. We had no acknowledgements because that was Mom's request.

"Charity suffereth long, and is kind; charity envieth not; charity vaunteth not itself, is not puffed up, Doth not behave itself unseemly, seeketh not her own, is not easily provoked, thinketh no evil." —1 Corinthians 13:4-5

Chapter 16

***

My Life without Mom

"Therefore the redeemed of the Lord shall return, and come with singing unto Zion; and everlasting joy shall be upon their head: they shall obtain gladness and joy; and sorrow and mourning shall flee away." —Isaiah 51:11

It has been over eleven years since my mother went home to glory. Yet when I look back on those days, I remember everything just like it was yesterday. The house felt so empty after the funeral and everyone left. Gloria stayed with George and me another week after Mom's funeral. It was good having her in the house. She did a lot to help me out. She cooked, cleaned, and washed clothes every day. She was like a busy little bee.

My mother's brother died three weeks after Mom. Even though it was difficult going to another funeral so soon, we supported the family. The months following the funeral were extremely stressful for me. I finally broke down and saw my doctor. After she checked me, she said that I was just plain exhausted. She said I had been so stressed during the time of my mother's illness that I couldn't fight anything off. I had over a year of rest to catch up with. Her advice was to let everything go until I felt better and to get some rest.

I took my doctor's advice. I got some rest and let everything else go until I felt like taking it on again. My mother is now in a better place. Losing her was without a doubt one of the most difficult things I have ever experienced. My mother told me often, "When I'm gone, you don't have to shed a tear over me because you have nothing to cry about. You were good to me. You were there when I needed you, and I thank you for everything." When I think about it, I realize that I *was* good to my mother. Nevertheless, I still cried a lot of tears. Even though I did everything within my power to make sure her needs were met, I am still human. Yes, life goes on, and we must cherish the memories. But it is so hard when you miss someone so much.

My grief was so heavy, and I felt such a loss that my entire being hurt. For weeks I stayed awake, night after night, going over in my mind every stage of Mom's sickness. Did I do all that I could have done? I thought about everything—her complaints, her medical appointments, different exams and tests, food I cooked for her, and her medication—*everything.*

There were also good thoughts as well. I thought about our long conversations at the table, in her room, and sitting outside. I thought of our car rides when she was able to go out for rides. I thought about taking her to see Miss Bell and Tracy. I thought about her excitement when she found out Stacy was retiring and moving home. Mom and I shared so many good memories. When I moved back to South Carolina in 2007, I started spending quite a bit of time with Mom. We were able to see each other often during that time. After she moved in with me, I was able to see her daily.

After Gloria left and returned to Connecticut, it was extremely difficult. The house felt so empty without Mom. I felt so alone and would cry at the drop of a hat. If someone so much as looked at me, I would cry. It didn't take much for the tears to fall. Walking in Mom's room would upset me. Sitting at the table alone would upset me. Mom was everywhere in my house. There were times when I could see her walking down the hallway, sitting outside under the carport, or walking in the yard. Yes, it was difficult. Thank God, Gloria helped me go through Mom's things before she left because I would not have been able to do it by myself. She knew exactly what was needed and she did it without even being asked.

They say that time heals all wounds. My mother and I made some good memories, and I will cherish them forever. I believe the love we have for a person remains there forever. Mom was a very special person to me, and I miss her so much. In fact, we all miss her dearly. Even though our hearts are filled with grief, we truly believe that she is in a better place. She was a good wife, mother, and friend, and we were blessed to have her in our lives as long as we did. I later sold that house and relocated back to Connecticut. George passed away May 7, 2020.

Yes we still have our moments, especially on her birthdays, Mother's Day and Christmas, but we will make it by the grace of God. Mom often said, "Don't worry about me – I'll be alright. I have made peace with God." We believe that she did make peace with God and was ready when He called her name.

Mom had this poem entitled "I'm Free" framed on her wall in Chesterfield. I took it down one day and read it. When I asked her where she got the poem, she said "David gave it to me." She loved this poem and so do I.

"I'm Free"

Don't grieve for me, for now I'm free
I'm following the path God has laid you see
I took His hand when I heard His call
I turned my back and left it all.
I could not stay another day
To laugh, to love, to work or play
Tasks left undone must stay that way
I found the peace at the close of day.
If my parting has left a void
Then fill it with remembered joys
A friendship shared, a laugh, a kiss
Oh yes, these things I too will miss.
Be not burdened with times of sorrow
I wish you the sunshine of tomorrow
My life's been full, I savored much:
Good friends, good times, a loved one's touch.
Perhaps my time seemed all to brief
Don't lengthen it now with undo grief
Lift up your heart, and peace to thee
God wanted me now, He set me free.

www.ingramcontent.com/pod-product-compliance
Lightning Source LLC
LaVergne TN
LVHW011931070526
838202LV00054B/4584